The Money Men

The Money Men

WILLIAM HAGGARD

WALKER AND COMPANY
NEW YORK

c. 1

M

First published in the United States of America
in 1981 by the Walker Publishing Company, Inc.

ISBN: 0-8027-5448-1

Library of Congress Catalog Card Number: 81-51974

Printed in the United States of America
10 9 8 7 6 5 4 3 2 1

Father Time is not always a
hard parent and, though he
tarries for none, often lays
his hand lightly on those
who have used him well.

Barnaby Rudge

1

He had been looking forward to this meeting with pleasure, for they had been something more than merely old friends. When he appeared before the Almighty in judgment Colonel Charles Russell, lately head of the Security Executive, could make one plea in mitigation: he had never left a woman to hate him. Molly Pegg had soon replaced him and he hadn't seen her for fifteen years. He wondered a little what she would look like. No doubt she would have put on some weight but she'd had the bonework to carry it and a fine high colouring. She would still have that pleasant Lowland burr which she'd been careful never to lose – it was useful – the brisk practical manner of the first-class officer, the easy and earthy approach to men. She was a Dame now, he reflected smiling, with honorary rank above his own. He would call her madam once and see what happened. Almost certainly she would stare and then laugh.

They had arranged to meet at his club for dinner. The service was not what once it had been, the food was sometimes a modest gamble, but the cellars still held some excellent wine and he'd remembered that next to honest venery Dame Molly loved good wine above all things. He was curious why she had telephoned suddenly. She was an unsentimental and down-to-earth woman and once an affair had ended accepted it. And one thing it would certainly not be, any question of financial embarrassment. She'd had some pretty rich lovers and some had been generous. Dame Molly had all the money she needed.

They drank a couple of sherries and then went upstairs. Charles Russell detested fuss with club waitresses, filling in an order blank and hoping it would reach someone literate, so he had ordered in advance and felt confident. The Dame ate smoked eel for he'd remembered she liked it and Russell himself had potted shrimps. With them they shared a fine Sauvignon. As a waiter cleared away for the woodcock Charles Russell asked her simply:

"What can I do?"

"Do you still have any financial connections?"

So it was money after all, he thought. He hid his surprise but a woman sensed it. Dame Molly said with her comfortable smile:

"No, it's not money – I've got enough. But I've been swindled and I'm a Lowland Scot."

"Better tell me the story."

She did so succinctly. It was the usual tale of the British abroad, the fiddle that wasn't precisely illegal and was therefore all the harder to tolerate. Her last lover had left her their flat in Chiavari which she'd immediately sold – she had loathed Chiavari – but she couldn't get the proceeds to England. The dollar premium had been properly paid, she had nothing to fear from Exchange Control, but the Italian bank wouldn't send her the money. She admitted she wasn't too clear why not but it was something to do with the original price. As was customary and indeed quite legal the price for the Italian tax which was exigible had been lower than the actual sum paid and the difference was being blocked in Italy. She had been to see an Italian lawyer, one whom the Consul had had on his list, but there'd been nothing much in it for him and he'd shown it. So back to the bank and the manager's sherry. Perfectly undrinkable, and worse than that he had demanded money. Of course it had been delicately done, but when the bush had been sufficiently beaten the animal which had emerged had been ugly. It had been four million Italian lire, say two thousand pounds in English money, over ten per cent of the price of the flat. And the man, though polite had been odiously sure of himself. He had said he'd be running a considerable risk, though he hadn't expressly said what risk, and in any case other English were amenable. He had obviously known the form.

Dame Molly had told him she'd see him in hell.

Charles Russell drank some Brouilly thoughtfully. He had heard this story more than once but had never been asked to take

8

a hand. Basically the solution was simple: you found somebody who wanted lire and for some reason didn't wish it known, then you wrote him a cheque on your Italian bank. The banker concerned might smell a rat but he wouldn't dare bounce a valid cheque made out to another account in Italy. Then the man who had taken your blocked lire refunded in another currency or better still he paid in notes. Irregular, of course, and awkward, since it wasn't the sort of deal to set up by a casual call on your branch of a clearing bank.

Russell started to shake his head but stopped. Dame Molly caught the gesture and laughed. "Half an idea?" she asked.

"A poor half." He noticed that her glass was empty. "A glass of wine?"

She looked at the bottle. "There isn't much left."

"There's another coming."

"May I use that as your epitaph?"

"Fine. But I mean to keep you waiting some time."

The wine came and a girl with the cheeseboard. She was the type Charles Russell thought of as 'Er-girl'. The Dame said: "I'd like some Brie, please."

"Er?"

Another man might have shown irritation but Russell merely pointed urbanely. "That one," he said. "A good big slice. And cut another for me if you will."

The Dame knew a lot about Russell and showed it, since when he wanted to think you must let him do so. She started on her Brie and kept silent.

For Russell had suddenly thought of Van Loon – old Van Loon who lived in Amsterdam. Like Dame Molly they hadn't connected for years, and their relationship hadn't been one of affection but the equal tie of a mutual interest. In the war a good banker had kept his head down. And after the peace he had helped Charles Russell, who had used him as a paymaster in an operation in Holland he had dared not acknowledge. Russell knew he was still a respected banker and he suspected he was extremely rich. The sum involved in Dame Molly's interest might sound to him like a simple impertinence.

In which case, Charles Russell thought, he could say so. He, Russell, was going to risk the snub for he'd been fonder of Molly Pegg than of most. She'd been swindled, which happened to most people sometime, but she was the type which took it extremely hard. She would fret and fume and that wouldn't be good for her.

"I think we've got an outside chance."

He gave her the background and she listened intently. "I would accept it in almost any money as long as those bloody Italians don't get it."

"Would Monday suit you?"

She looked at a diary. "Suit me for what?"

"To fly to Amsterdam to see Van Loon."

"You think I should come too?"

"Of course. There's nothing like solid corroboration."

"There and back in a day?"

"I don't see why not."

"I've nothing I can't put off."

"That's good. Then I'll ring Van Loon and ask for a meeting. That I'm pretty sure he won't refuse. I'll also get the tickets and let you know. It will have to be an early flight. After eleven o'clock in the morning elderly men are inclined to deteriorate."

The flight had for once been smooth and comfortable. No air controller was throwing a tantrum, no loader had been dismissed for theft and his fellows gone on strike in protest. It had been almost like that quickie on the box – stewardess putting rug round old lady. One of them had tried it on Molly and had been spoken to with a certain acerbity. Russell drank coffee, surprisingly good, and afterwards lit a cigarette. He didn't often smoke cigarettes but knew that cigars were not acceptable. Dame Molly Pegg who was watching her weight drank tea with lemon and made a face.

At Schiphol they took the first taxi they saw for they hadn't a great deal of time to fritter. Russell gave the address in a street near the Vondelpark, and when they arrived climbed down and looked round him. He had been here before but a long time ago and could see that the quarter had changed considerably. The same fine old houses still stood intact, once the homes of the city's rich bourgeoisie, but now most of them were smallish hotels of the kind which Russell much preferred to the pompous caravanserai which disfigured the city's once proud centre. A few were still houses in private possession. They went up the steps of one of these and rang the bell.

They were shown at once into old Van Loon's study. The men shook hands with a quiet formality and old Van Loon bowed to Molly Pegg. There were two chairs before a mahogany desk and the old man made a gesture towards them. They sat down and he went to his own chair behind it. He walked with sticks and very slowly, and when he sat down it was clear that it hurt him. He didn't ask them their business; he sat impassive.

It had been agreed that Molly should tell the story and Russell had time to inspect Van Loon. He was eighty-five at least and probably more. His head was as bald as a billiard-ball but his fine eyebrows were black over hooded eyes. His hands were beautifully kept and he held them still. Behind him on the wall was a painting. Charles Russell thought the frame too heavy but it was expertly lighted, as Dutch as Gouda. Russell guessed it as a good Vermeer. The old man caught his glance and smiled.

"A copy, of course, but a very good one. The original disappeared in the war."

Dame Molly told her story simply and the old man listened without interruption. The amount involved was no more than peanuts and the transaction would be perfectly simple. There were half a dozen rich men in Holland who would be glad of such a sum in Italy but less glad to have it transferred there openly. They would pay him in guilders or pounds and be happy to. But he was cautious as his profession dictated and he didn't make an immediate promise.

"You will realise I take little part in business but I will leave a note for my son with some optimism." He turned to Russell. "I don't think you've met him." It was clear he was changing the subject deliberately. On the proposition before him he'd said all that he wished to but it wouldn't be polite just to rise.

"No," Russell said, "that's a pleasure to come."

In this he was entirely mistaken.

"He has a villa in Estoril, you see, and has gone there to look at some alterations." The old man hesitated but then went on. "When I'm dead I suspect he'll live there permanently."

This was news to Russell and he didn't mind showing it. "But the business – "

"I doubt if my son cares much for the business."

Russell sensed that this was at best a half-truth and his instinct was to stop talking at once. But he looked at Van Loon and changed his mind. The impassive old face had somehow lightened, the hoods on the eyes had lifted, he was alive. Talking freely to strangers was doing him good. Very likely he had few friends to talk to and almost certainly fewer contemporaries.

Charles Russell put out another feeler. "Then your grandsons perhaps – "

"I have no grandsons." For a moment the old man stopped again, then went on in a sort of reluctant rush. "Nor likely now to see one born. My son, you see, has never married."

He was looking at Molly Pegg as he spoke and Molly could read his message. He wasn't telling her his son was bent, he was telling her he wasn't interested. She knew more medicine than many doctors and the jargon came into her mind at once . . . Low Testicular Activity. Ha! She was genuinely sorry for Mijnheer Van Loon. He had built up a considerable House and then to beget a neuter! Disaster.

Russell looked again at Van Loon; he could see he was tiring. The sudden surge of candour had done him good but the price would be a powerful reaction. Charles Russell too could read Van Loon though he read him on a different wavelength. He knew what he wanted, he wanted his gin, and he didn't wish to drink in company. A servant would help him to reach his armchair and another would bring a bottle of Oudemeester and maybe a little water in a jug.

Charles Russell nodded at Molly, who rose. "I don't know how to thank you."

"Do not. Recollect that I have made no promises." A thought

seemed to strike him; he rubbed his chin. "Any preference in regard to currency?"

"Anything but Indian rupees."

For the first time the old man allowed a smile. "I understand you perfectly, madam." They protested but he struggled upright. He rang a bell and a servant showed them out.

In the taxi back to the airport Russell was silent. Dame Molly Pegg made a single remark.

"And to think I've sometimes envied the rich."

From the front of the returning aircraft a young man had come up to them smiling. "Good morning, sir," he said to Russell.

"Good morning, Willy. What are you doing here?"

"Keeping an eye on you as it happens."

Charles Russell was surprised but concealed it. He made the introductions smoothly. "Dame Molly Pegg, William Wilberforce Smith." Willy Smith wore quiet but expensive clothes and his manners were those of a man rather older, cool and unselfconsciously confident. He bowed to Dame Molly Pegg politely and when she smiled, but not before, gave her his own which was wide and handsome. He had very white teeth and he showed them generously. Against his black skin the effect was electric. Black but comely, Molly privately thought. A killer if you happened to fancy them.

The meal had been served, the trays removed, and for a moment the aisle of the aircraft was empty. They could chat without Willy becoming a nuisance.

"I think you said you were keeping an eye on me. That could mean one of two things. Please explain."

"As it happens I was doing a tail."

Russell was surprised again and this time didn't bother to hide it. He knew that he wasn't shadowed regularly so there must be some specific reason. Willy Smith read his thought and expressed it frankly. "You're not shadowed in England but you may be abroad. Sir Richard has never quite learnt to accept you."

Richard Laver was Charles Russell's successor in the hot seat of the Security Executive. He'd been a political choice and not Russell's own.

"But should you be telling me this?"

"No, of course not."

A woman came down the aisle with a screaming child, and whilst she alternately bullied and pleaded, the dialogue had to end abruptly. The break was welcome to Russell for he needed to think.

What Willy was doing was wildly irregular. Tails didn't walk up to their quarries and wish them Good Day; they didn't announce who had given them orders nor delicately suggest that those orders were foolish. William Wilberforce Smith had done all three.

Well, he'd always been Russell's man, his disciple. Russell had recruited him and had never had cause to regret the appointment. Willy could go where a white could not, though his own background was well removed from criminal. He was a West Indian but comfortably off, for his grandfather had made a considerable fortune, partly by rack-renting other West Indians and partly by running a chain of brothels, the discreet sort of brothel which in South London was once tolerated. The police had more important duties and if money sometimes passed at Christmas, that too was a matter for proper discretion. Willy Smith had been bright and his father ambitious. After Harrow he had suggested the army, and the suggestion had been seriously considered. With Harrow behind him and a generous allowance there were regiments which would have taken him gladly, not simply to show they weren't conscious of colour but as an officer they would be pleased to have.

But Willy hadn't fancied the army. It might be tolerable in war, he had thought, but he wasn't going to get shot in Ulster, one hand tied behind him by nervous politicos. He had drifted for a time in the City, then a banker friend of Russell had noticed him, noticed that he was drifting and wondered ...

And now here he was still but working for Laver. The woman had somehow subdued the child and they could talk again, though not in comfort.

"Aren't you being a little indiscreet?"

"Not with my late respected master."

Russell had no ready answer to that and they were getting on ground he didn't fancy. He said since it offered a fair retreat:

"May I ask what you'll tell your present master?"

"I shall dutifully report what I know. Which is that you went to Amsterdam, accompanied, and that you called at the house of one Van Loon who I happen to know is a well-known, well, banker. After that you returned on this aircraft, drinking two gins."

"And what will Laver make of that?"

"I haven't an idea what he'll make of it."

It had been spoken with something not far from contempt and Russell was at once uneasy. He had suspected that Willy Smith and Laver were not hitting it off as he'd genuinely hoped they would, and he could make an embarrassing guess why not.

But Willy, if asked, would have told him simply. Russell had handled him right and Laver hadn't. When he'd made mistakes – to start with many – Russell had reprimanded him mercilessly; he had made no allowances, none whatever; he'd been totally unconscious of colour. But Laver was always making allowances and he did it in the worst way possible. Behind the bland mask of liberal humanism were words which were never spoken but always there ... "Of course I can see you're black and I'm white but you must never think that makes the least difference." But it did make a difference, a deadly distinction. There was patronage here, though entirely unconscious. Open patronage he would have shrugged off indifferently. He had been to a better school than Laver; he'd be richer and he had better manners. It was the tedious conscientious effort to suppress a judgment always present which William Wilberforce Smith resented. For Richard Laver he would do his duty but for Russell he'd do a great deal more.

They had started on the routine of landing and a stewardess came up to Willy. "Will you please sit down, sir, and fasten your seat belt." Willy smiled at Russell and bowed to Dame Molly. When he was out of earshot she said:

15

"I like your friend. He's a bit of a charmer."

Russell didn't answer her. A vestigial instinct warned that something was wrong but he buried it under a rigid discipline. He was doing a job for Dame Molly Pegg, he was retired and enjoying retirement sensibly. He hadn't been retired with grace and occasionally, in the small hours, felt bitter. But he wasn't going to replay old hands. Post-mortems at bridge had always bored him.

Karel van Loon returned to Holland the day after Russell left with Dame Molly. He went first to his office and spent three hours there for even a week away had meant arrears. Then an office car took him home to the Vondelpark. The splendid old house was now two flats. Karel van Loon was living in one and his father, with a daily male nurse, had preferred to end his life in the other. Once a day they took a meal together but otherwise they lived apart. The cooking was done from a single kitchen. There was a Javanese cook who made fine *rijsttafel* and three elderly maids who lived in the attics. Domestic service, in Holland, was not yet unheard of though you needed to be rich to employ it.

Karel van Loon went first to his study. On his desk was a brief note from his father, written in the old man's spidery hand. It was expressed as a request, not an order, but there was a feeling that if it wasn't complied with the old man would need an excellent reason. There was a certain sum which was blocked in Italy. The amount and the names of the bank and account-holder he would find on a separate piece of paper, together with that of a friend of his father who had introduced the business in question. His father would like to oblige this friend so he wished the money brought back to Holland. After that any transfer would be a simple routine. Commission would in this case be waived.

It was as succinct as a military order.

Van Loon looked at the separate paper and frowned. The money involved was inconsiderable, hardly worth the trouble of trading in even if commission had not been waived. But he was a dutiful son if not an affectionate, and he had often heard the

16

name of Charles Russell. He and his father had been close in the war and the Englishman was now using his contact. One day there might be a quid pro quo. To a good Dutchman that was too good to miss.

He went down and knocked on his father's door for they'd arranged to dine together that evening. His father would want to know about Estoril. He disapproved of the project to transfer the business there (for that was the story his son had given him) but his resistance had been surprisingly mild and his heir believed he knew the reason. He hadn't succeeded in founding a family and there were persuasive fiscal reasons for the move.

Also others which his son hadn't told him.

So he knocked on his father's door. No one answered. His father would be napping. He hesitated. Finally he went in quietly. His father was in his usual chair, but he wasn't napping. His father was dead. He rocked him gently. His head fell lower.

Van Loon was shocked but not extravagantly. His father was very old and frail, at the end of a series of crippling heart attacks. Moreover he was defying his doctors. He still drank gin, half a bottle a day, and he still smoked the long pale cheroots he loved. One had fallen from his hand at this moment, burning a hole in a fine Kubas rug. Van Loon picked it up and trod out the burn. The rug was ruined, though. A pity. It was worth a couple of thousand pounds.

He sat down to consider for he wasn't quite satisfied. He had already had two threats to abduct him, and on the form in the rest of the world at the moment they were something which he took very seriously. But he had never considered his father in danger. At his age he'd be an untempting target. But it was conceivable he could be killed as a warning.

The old man had died with his bottle of Oudemeester and Van Loon got up and smelt it carefully. It smelt, as he had expected, of gin. He sat down again, a little ashamed, for the action had been a suspicious reflex. Poison would be a stupid crudity and international gangs of extortioners were anything in their methods but crude. His father was an old man who'd had several strokes. Any man with a modest medical knowledge could have finished him without leaving a trace. Some sudden shock or a knowing pressure and there'd be nothing for the cleverest policeman.

Besides, to go to the police would be most unwise. He couldn't be sure of cooperation.

He made up his mind and sent for Jan, the male nurse.

"I think my father is dead. I'd like you to come."

The male nurse arrived in twenty minutes. His father had fled the Nazi terror. A widower, he'd brought his young son with him and had somehow managed to make a living till the Occupation had ended that. He had gone into hiding but the Gestapo had found him, as they'd found many who had been quietly betrayed. They had sent him back to Germany to a work camp where he'd been starved to death. Jan had been only a child, they had left him, but he still spoke Dutch with a German accent.

He examined his master and closed his eyes. As he straightened he looked at the bottle and shrugged.

"I'd have done the same," Van Loon said softly. What use was three more months of life deprived of your only remaining pleasures? He asked the nurse:

"When did the doctor last see him?"

"Yesterday."

"Then there needn't be an inquest?"

"No. That being so we should take him away."

They carried old Van Loon to his bedroom. He was surprisingly light, for the strokes had wasted him. They put him on his bed and Van Loon locked the door.

"I don't think I need detain you. Good night."

He went back to the study and made the arrangements; the doctor to give a straightforward certificate and an undertaker to manage the funeral. It was going to be a simple one, for his father had always detested pomp and in any case there were few relations. Karel van Loon was the last of his line.

He looked at the fine Vermeer and smiled. It wasn't the copy his father had called it and its history was a long way from creditable.

He went to bed but not to sleep, considering the new situation. He had respected his father but loved him little. He'd been a

18

man of a different age and mores, a Calvinist, fiercely upright and grim. Van Loon had often thought his standards too high. He regretted his death but it was undeniably convenient.

For he couldn't have fled to Estoril with his father alive in Holland behind him. Not as he meant to flee, with everything. The proposition had been to move the business to a country which now gave unlimited scope for it, but that hadn't been all of the truth – far from it.

For Van Loon was going to play it dirty; Van Loon intended to run with the lot. What was legally his, what he held for others. That is, if those other bastards let him.

William Wilberforce Smith was giving her dinner, Amanda Dee whom he meant to marry. Her parents were even richer than his and she'd been educated in the strictest propriety, a convent, though her parents were Baptist, and then a fashionable finishing school. There was a tall old house near Clapham Common, and rather to the south of that Amanda was ribaldly called 'the Princess'. He could see that she wasn't particularly pretty but he thought her a very smart chick indeed.

She was helplessly in love with him but knew that to show it too openly wouldn't be wise. But she looked at him and shivered deliciously. His face was Nilotic rather than African, his eyelids with the sensuous curve which she had seen in museums in tribal carvings; his mouth wasn't fleshy, his ears were small. A Zulu, she thought – he could well be a Zulu. The old Arab slavers had greatly prized them and some long-suppressed gene had suddenly sprouted.

He was normally debonnaire and talked easily but this evening he was unusually silent. She asked him why and he told her simply:

"Boss trouble," he said, "and it's getting worse."

She didn't like the sound of that. He was far too well trained to be indiscreet but was permitted to say that he 'worked in Security'. That didn't matter to her but it did to her father: it put Willy on her father's short list. There weren't many men she could acceptably marry since her parents were not only rich but choosey. They couldn't have their daughter marrying what they considered beneath her.

"What sort of trouble? You're getting the sack?" That would be a complete disaster. Harrow and Butterfly cricket would not be enough. He would have money still and so would she, but her father had strict and old-fashioned values. A man had a job or a man was nothing, and the man who married Amanda Dee must have a job in which he could hold his head up.

But Willy laughed. "Not as bad as that. Not yet."

She was relieved but said only: "Why not tell me?"

"It's difficult – sort of inside out. If he bullied me I'd walk out at once and if he patronised me I could laugh it off. But he treats me as though I wasn't a person, just an exercise in race relations."

"I know what you mean, I've sometimes seen it. The better intentioned they are – "

"You've got it!"

She was really a smart chick, a flyer. "And he's still a little jealous of Russell."

"What sort of man is he?"

"Not quite our class."

Amanda nodded; she understood. The words might be snobbish but not Willy Smith. It was simply that in their own seething society class distinctions were extremely important. That might be deplorable, maybe it wasn't, but to state the fact simply without fumbling apology made no man any sort of stuffed shirt.

When they'd finished their coffee he escorted her home. She would have liked to dance but he didn't suggest it. There were discos by dozens but most were rowdy, and one didn't take the local princess to a place where there might be a fight or worse. He wasn't afraid of a fight – not at all – but he was a little afraid of Amanda's father. He was one generation ahead of his own and apart from his money that gave him much standing. His grandfather had gone into private service where he had picked up a working knowledge of silver. His master had left him a modest legacy and on it he had started a jeweller's. He'd sold mostly trash to the eager locals but the occasional good piece as well as the old Victorian houses broke up in the rising flood of immigration. Now Amanda's father, his grandson, had a chain of them, one specialising still in silver. It had a very good name and sold only the best.

Willy Smith stopped the taxi and handed her out. The house was one of the very few which were still in single occupation: the others were flats or second-class offices. Her father could well have afforded to move but he'd been born in this house and preferred to die there. In every instinct he was entirely conservative.

They went up the ugly stone steps to the door and at it she raised her face. They kissed chastely. She didn't ask him in since she didn't dare.

Willy went back to his taxi thoughtfully. He'd marry her since both parents approved of it but he could wish that she wasn't quite such an iceberg.

Amanda went up to her room and lay down. She cried a little but not very much. It was a pity he was quite such a dumbo. If he'd asked her to let down a couple of sheets she would have helped him up and accepted the consequences.

2

Sir Richard Laver of the Security Executive read Willy Smith's brief note with annoyance. He had been appointed to succeed Charles Russell in circumstances which had been somewhat unusual and there were people who thought they'd been actively shabby. Charles Russell hadn't been sacked or squeezed out but nor had he been encouraged to stay. There had recently been a change of government but Russell's post was apolitical and he himself had always been scrupulous. Too scrupulous and that had undone him. A major political scandal had broken and the international implications had necessarily involved the Executive. The new Prime Minister had made his mind clear; he wanted the maximum smother possible. Charles Russell had disagreed and said so. People were entitled to know that the country had utterly ruthless enemies. He hadn't done a thing he shouldn't, he hadn't leaked a word to the Press, but nor had he lifted a finger to fluff it. The Prime Minister had not been pleased for the scandal had cost him a string of by-elections. Charles Russell, who wasn't a civil servant, was on a contract which hadn't long to run and when it expired it was not renewed.

He was not surprised and departed quietly but there was astonishment in several countries. He had an international reputation and here were the British letting him go. There were other signs and ominous portents that the British were bent on self-destruction but to the hard men of the world's secret services the action seemed one of total folly. The British Prime Minister didn't think so and he was aware of Russell's reputation. So he not only let him go, he gave orders. Charles Russell was far too scrupulous to be an embarrassment in internal politics but if he should wish to work abroad – advisory of course, not executive – there was one country in particular which would simply ask him to name his terms. That *would* be an embarrassment and the Prime Minister was a cautious man, his party a ragbag of warring factions. Richard Laver had been his personal choice, an efficient and orthodox civil servant, precisely what the Prime Minister wanted after the cool panache of Colonel Charles Russell. He told Laver what to do in person. In England it wasn't worth watching Russell, but when he went abroad and he went quite often the Prime Minister was to be told at once, in particular of any political contact.

So Laver read Willy Smith with annoyance since he gave him that most difficult task, to write a report on nothing which didn't sound silly. His standing orders had been mandatory – *any* visit abroad, any visit whatever – and he wasn't a man to ignore an order. But the Prime Minister could be irascible, especially when pestered with tedious trifles, and if any visit abroad looked innocent this one stood very high on the list.

Laver read Willy's paper again and frowned. Charles Russell and Dame Molly Pegg; they had called on old Van Loon and at once returned. Laver had heard of Van Loons – it was puzzling. Ostensibly they were merchant bankers but their real business was hiding rich men's money. He knew that they had some surprising clients, including that loud-mouthed Leftie bishop who prated of the Church's commitment. But you had to be pretty rich to use them, half a million at least he'd have guessed if he'd had to, and neither Russell nor Molly Pegg had that money.

He corrected himself for he wasn't sure. He knew only that Russell had modest means but it was possible that he'd inherited more. Then why take Molly Pegg? For the trip? Laver knew that they had once been lovers – he kept a thickish file on the late head of the Executive – but they'd returned the same day and immediately parted. So there was only one hypothesis which covered the few facts which were known: one of her boyfriends had left Molly a fortune and she had gone to an old flame, Russell, for advice. The evidence was inconclusive but there was another perhaps related fact which supported the web of inference strongly. Laver had read Charles Russell's file carefully and he knew that he'd once before used Van Loons. Some matter in the war, he remembered. Then there you were with a previous contact. Charles Russell had used it perfectly innocently.

He wrote a note for the Prime Minister's eyes alone. He wrote standard First Division Mandarin, lucid but as flat as a puncture, ideally designed to conceal the fact that the writer was saying nothing whatever. He didn't think much of the note himself, but the Prime Minister had been clear and insistent. Any visit abroad, any visit whatever.

Laver addressed an envelope carefully. *The Right Honourable Alistair Leech, P.C., M.P.* He looked at it with an acid smile for he knew that the name embarrassed its owner. He would insist it was of Celtic origin, pronounced somewhat like a Scottish lake, then drift into a dissertation on how P Celts could understand Breton but Q Celts could not. It was a practised act in intimate circles but unsuitable for public performance. There he had to face the sniggers. He had a pachyderm's skin and could do so equably but privately he wasn't happy. The name had unfortunate contemporary overtones, and sniggers, in the pinches, could cost a man votes.

Laver marked the envelope SECRET – it wasn't – and lit his fiftieth cigarette. He smoked far too many but couldn't unhook. He was pleased the affair had turned out to be nothing, but at a deeper level was faintly regretful. It wouldn't entirely have displeased him if Russell had found himself in trouble. Consciously he felt obliged to admire him but behind all that was a certain malice. For Russell had everything Laver hadn't, the urbanity and the great reputation; he had made it all look absurdly easy. What Laver must do with a conscious effort Russell had seemed to sail through casually. Laver had never analysed this; he didn't believe in deep-down-delving since you never quite knew what the net might dredge up.

It might even bring up his suppressed resentment, his envy if he were forced to face it.

On an impulse he sent for William Wilberforce Smith. "Good morning, Smith."

24

"Good morning, sir."

Laver waved at a chair. "Please sit down. Is there anything from Holland recently?"

"We've a stringer there but he reports to you."

"I meant from Jane Lightwater."

"Not that I've heard of."

Jane Lightwater was a high-class tart who specialised in diplomats and the wealthy visiting business men they brought to her. She was particular and her fees were enormous. On top of those the Security Executive paid her a weekly retainer for what she picked up. For months on end it was only gossip but every now and then she hit gold. Willy Smith was the weekly contact between them.

"When did you last see her, then?"

"Last Thursday. It's her regular pay day."

"And today is only Monday. A pity." Laver considered, then added deliberately: "I'd be greatly obliged if you'd call today."

Willy Smith thought the words unnecessarily formal. Charles Russell would simply have said: "Go today."

"What is she to look out for, please?"

"I'm interested at the moment in Holland. One of her clients is high up in their embassy."

"Wouldn't our stringer do better from Amsterdam?"

"No." Richard Laver was distinctly put out. He disliked being taught his business by juniors. Any other he would have promptly bitten but felt a duty to keep his teeth out of Willy. He controlled his irritation sharply and repeated, this time more smoothly:

"No. The stringer covers the politics and he does it, as you know, very well."

. . . Why doesn't he come to the point and spill it?

"Then what sort of story is Jane to look out for?"

"Anything financial."

"Such as Van Loons?"

Richard Laver flushed but again controlled himself. It wasn't this young man's business to question him but again he felt that his hands were tied. He hated the restraint in secret but felt he

25

was compelled to honour it. He thought again and then said reasonably:

"I can see I had better be perfectly frank."

... Like hell you will be perfectly frank.

"I've a suspicion about Van Loons – a grave one."

"And Jane is to smell about for the body?"

"You could put it like that."

"I'll do just as you say." Willy Smith thought in turn; he was going to risk it. He knew that Richard Laver disliked him but also that in his way he was scared of him. Enough scared not to dismiss him out of hand.

"And anything on Colonel Russell?"

Laver rose at once to end the interview; he said in his most official manner:

"I consider you are exceeding your duties."

When Willy had gone Richard Laver thought huffily. He was resentful of Russell's reputation but even more that Willy Smith adored him. Smith was his, Richard Laver's servant, yet he walked at Russell's heel like a dog. It was galling, it nagged like an unripe gumboil.

Willy walked to Jane Lightwater's flat with a smile. He walked because he needed exercise. Ordinarily he took it in cricket but they had been shorthanded in the office lately and he hadn't been able to get away. He liked Jane Lightwater and looked forward to meeting her.

The smile changed to a friendly grin as he remembered what he had learnt at school.

When Lady Jane became a tart
It nearly broke her father's heart

There followed some lines of indifferent doggerel and then the punch lines, brisk and startling.

So he bought her the most exclusive beat
On the sunny side of Jermyn Street

Except that he had done no such thing. Jane had never walked in her life. She was expensive and she was also choosey. Her number was on no head porter's list: you had to be properly introduced and even then she might turn you down. So Willy flogged on up the Edgware Road, wondering why she chose to live there. She could have afforded to live much further north, but he'd guessed that the neighbours would put her off, the sub-intelligentsia on inherited money, fringe publishing and work in hospitals. Not nursing, of course – that was much too strenuous and they'd be disciplined by no-nonsense matrons – but handing out novels and tea and sympathy. The men were trying to write books or sell pictures. A very few had productive jobs and those who had were despised by the others. The scrape of the scratching of backs was incessant.

Willy turned right and came to her block of flats. It was a fair address but not a grand one. He had telephoned and she let him in. She wasn't dressed like a whore expecting custom but in admirable country tweeds. Her shoes were well kept, her hair even better. She had told him her ambition once, which was a small village house in some market town and a couple of hacks to pass the time. He had guessed that she was quite close to her target. From time to time she might take a lover but she probably wouldn't marry again. Not unless there were real advantages.

"Mr William Smith."

"Mrs Jane Lightwater."

They always began with extreme formality. It was a part of their game and both enjoyed it.

He handed her her weekly envelope but she put it on one side unopened. "I'm early this week but I'm looking for news."

A natural question would have been "Of what?" but her profession had taught her never to hurry. She sat him down, poured him ginger ale since he seldom drank, and a very small whisky indeed for herself. She returned to her own chair and waited, thinking how handsome he looked in those beautiful clothes. He had never made the faintest pass at her though once or twice she herself had been tempted. She supposed that he didn't fancy white women. Perhaps he knew too much about them.

Eventually she prompted him gently. "What sort of news do you want me to get you?"

"News from the Netherlands. Do you still see that old Yonkheer of yours?"

"He only comes about once a month and even then he isn't much good but I do see the business friend he brought with him."

"Has he told you what his business is?"

"Piet said he was a banker."

"What sort?"

"Is there more than one sort?"

"Indeed there is." He seemed to be changing the subject abruptly. "Have you heard of the Bishop of Crondal?"

"Yes." A High Anglican herself she loathed him.

"Well, in the intervals of preaching socialism he hides a large fortune abroad in Europe where his left-wing friends can't get a touch of it."

"In a numbered account?"

"No, that's rather old hat. There are better ways of doing it now and the people concerned tend to cluster in Holland."

"You'd better start at the beginning," she said.

"Then you'll remember I spent some time in the City. I worked in a merchant bank as it happened, and there I managed to learn rather more than I should have counting notes in a clearing bank. I learnt something of how the rich hide their money. You remember Goering and that disreputable trial, all the king's horses and all the king's lawyers inventing the law as they went along?"

"You mean Nuremberg?"

Willy nodded. "Goering died in some mystery before they could hang him and they never got all of his loot. Not all of it. They got the jewellery and furniture and most of the pictures – he'd been partial to stout nudes in woods – but his bank account was suspiciously small. They traced the money to Spain and that was that. Nobody could do a thing, not even the Custodians of Enemy Property and they were the hardest hombres within the law. Spain was a neutral country, you see, and the Nazi had given his money away. He had *given* it to a Spanish nobleman, who wouldn't have dared not to give it back if Germany had won the war. But Germany didn't win the war. The Nazi was dead and there was the money, all in the Spaniard's name, quite legally. He is now an enormously wealthy man."

"But that was just after the war."

"I know. But the principle is still the same. Take the Bishop of Crondal of evil omen; he uses a Dutch house called Van Loons."

"You mean they hold that Leftie's money?"

"Not *hold* his money, they don't hold a thing. They're not trustees. They *own* his money."

She put her finger on the essential at once. "You mean that they could lift the lot?"

"I mean just that."

"Well, I'll be damned."

"But of course they don't, they would hardly dare. This is Big Business in largish capitals and there is more than one specialist house which does it. One default would blow the whole racket wide open, so honesty is for once the best policy. The State wouldn't like a run-out either: these businesses bring in a lot of lolly. No doubt there'll be a bad egg sometime – there always is when you come to think of it – but so far nobody's broken the rules."

She brought him another ginger ale; she had a quick brain and had grasped it quickly. "I think I've got the banking side, bizarre as the whole story sounds. But what does the depositor get, our deplorable bishop to take your example? What does the hander-over get apart from the risk that he'll lose his money?"

"He avoids any tax, for example."

"How?"

"Van Loons or whoever he's using buy bearers. They collect the interest and bring it over in cash."

"Sounds risky."

"Very little risk. There's a hatful of flights between Holland and England and they don't use the same runner every time. And it isn't only income tax at which you can now raise two fingers happily. When you die you pay no capital transfer tax."

"Hasn't the Inland Revenue rumbled it?"

"I'm sure they have but it isn't easy for them. They have to operate under the law or get rapped. And the law is heavily on your side. You're no longer the formal legal owner, and since Van Loons are not trustees you're not what's called the beneficial." Willy Smith smiled widely: the situation amused him. "Somebody is sending you presents. That is, whilst you're alive to receive them."

"And when you're dead?"

"It depends how you've fixed it. The usual arrangement is children and siblings and after that Van Loons take the money. I dare say you could negotiate longer but the charges would be correspondingly higher. It's not an arrangement for men with large families or men who want to found a dynasty. But for rich men who want to live as they did it's a fiddle with very attractive advantages. Of course it isn't entirely watertight – no fiddle is really ever quite that – but the odds are pretty good in your favour."

"And the Bishop of Crondal has no children."

"Of course he hasn't, he's bent almost double."

She laughed. "That's a very clear background – I think I've got it. It's hard to believe but you say it happens." She was suddenly brisk and entirely businesslike. "Now what do you want me to do?"

"I'll tell you. That banker of yours – do you see him often?"

She looked at a well-filled diary. "Later this week."

"I'd like you to make him talk."

"I'll do that all right – the man's in love with me. But I need to know what about."

"Here it comes," Willy said; he collected his thoughts. "I mentioned Van Loons because Van Loons are in point. It's suspected that something is cooking in Holland, perhaps some big financial scandal, and if it were Van Loons we've an interest. Not in what they do but for whom."

He had constructed this little speech with some care for in fact there were two suspicions, not one. Laver suspected that something was brewing; he was perfectly entitled to that. But Willy suspected Laver's motives and that he had no right to do. He was Charles Russell's man but Laver's employee. On an aircraft he had disclosed his business there but he didn't consider that mortal sin. He was easily identifiable and Russell might have noticed him anyway; he might have wondered and made two and two five. So that hadn't been a dereliction, but it would be an outrage to say to Jane Lightwater straightly: "I suspect that my present boss hates my former."

But Jane who knew nothing of this was following up. "I think I get it – the smell of a bust-up. Particularly if it affects Van Loons. Can I mention Van Loons?"

He considered that carefully. "You can if you must but it's more convincing if your banker friend drops the name himself. When are you going to see him, by the way?"

She looked at the diary again. "On Friday."

"That's quite a long time. Could you ring him up?"

"That would be unprofessional. No." She had spoken with a certain severity but also with a sort of wry humour. They both of them laughed.

"So I'll have to wait till Friday."

"I'm sorry."

But he didn't have to wait till Friday for she rang him the following morning, waking him up.

"William Wilberforce Smith."

"Mrs Jane Lightwater."

"Piet turned up last night unexpectedly. It was very inconvenient and I had to juggle the timetable madly." The matter-of-fact voice changed to banter. "But you know that I'd do anything for you."

And for a hundred and twenty a week, he thought. But all he said was simply:

"Yes?"

"It's yes, all right – he talked and talked. I gave him the works and he couldn't stop."

"I bet he couldn't."

"Willy, you've got a dirty mind. I was afraid he was going to throw a coronary, but he didn't, he got home in one piece. That was good since I'm rather fond of Piet."

She was in very good form and he waited patiently. "And it's very much as you thought it was. He mentioned Van Loons without my having to, and Van Loons are on the hot seat properly. They're not going bust – no, nothing like that – but Karel van Loon is being threatened."

"Did your friend say by whom?"

"He didn't know. But the rumour is that they're pretty big boys."

"And the reason for the threats?"

"A blank."

"Never mind," he said. "I can only thank you."

"Any other time."

"Good hunting."

3

Karel van Loon was re-reading his father's Will. The Van Loons had owned only distant cousins and to these the old man had left proper remembrances, plus two thousand pounds to his faithful male nurse. His son rang his lodging and a woman's voice answered.

"I'd like to speak to Jan, if I may."

"I'm afraid he isn't here, Mijnheer."

"Can you say when he'll be back?"

"I cannot."

"But surely – "

"I mean he has gone; he has disappeared. He has taken his clothes and the few things he had with him. Last night he was here and this morning he isn't. He didn't leave any message or even address."

"Was there any trouble? Did he owe you money?"

"He owed a week's rent but he left that behind him."

"But no address, you say?"

"No, none."

Van Loon was vexed since this meant delay. He was naturally his father's executor and he wanted his legal discharge on the dot. He rang his lawyers but they weren't over-helpful. There would have to be the fullest enquiries but after a certain time he could lodge a bond. How much delay? Hard to say but there was bound to be some.

Delay suited Van Loon in no way whatever. His father had told Dame Molly Pegg of a villa in Portugal which perhaps he would move to, and his father's remark had in fact been prescient. For Van Loon was being threatened remorselessly and in Portugal he could make arrangements which in Holland would be out of the question.

On his last trip Karel van Loon had made several. The first had been with the local police who had smiled unbelievingly but had accepted his money. The Villa Fleury was large with a porter's lodge and they had found him a suitable man to live in it, an ex-hoodlum who was now going straight. The villa, too, would need alterations to turn it into the fortress he needed, for he had no illusions that simple menaces couldn't turn into something a great deal severer. He wasn't some minor civil servant who had once slipped from grace and was now being blackmailed; he was a very rich man and a tempting target. It happened in parts of Europe every week. It was a snatch he was afraid of – abduction. Kidnapping and then self-ransom. His distant cousins were not well off, so he'd be out on his own, victim rather than hostage. They would take him for every guilder he had, and if he resisted they would administer pain with the clinical precision of doctors. It was better to lie low for a year and after that he would see what happened.

But he needed a safe house to do it and was turning the Villa Fleury into one. The tall hedge was being backed by wire netting and that netting could be electrified nightly. The cellar was being made a strong room for he didn't intend to leave much behind him. Already he'd moved out most of the bearers. Willy Smith had been right: he had plenty of couriers. They lay for the moment in a Portuguese bank, at risk to some international law suit, but this wasn't one which he meant to run long. His gold had been sold at the top of the market. Only the fine Vermeer remained and that would need expert handling and packing. When the time came he'd run that out himself, hiding it in his car and chancing it. For the moment there was nothing more; he must wait on the Portuguese contractors. They weren't quite as bad as the neighbouring Spaniards but they were difficult to keep to schedule. Difficult? They had proved impossible.

But there were two things he could do from his desk and one of them he did immediately. He rang up a firm of private enquiry agents and asked for a rundown on Jan, the male nurse.

34

The other was a little less simple and needed an act of conscious judgment. He turned from the Will to other papers, noticing a letter from Italy. Dame Molly's account had been satisfactorily closed and an equivalent sum was now banked in Rotterdam to the order of Mijnheer Karel van Loon. To Karel van Loon the transaction had been trifling, especially when done without commission, but it had been his father's instruction and he had decided to honour it. Besides, he thought, with his banker's smile, it was Charles Russell who had introduced Dame Molly, and one could never tell when a man like Russell might not somehow, somewhere turn out to be useful. And it was Russell that he was to deliver the money.

He looked at another paper and nodded. He had many other clients in Britain besides a bishop whom he considered insane and several were coming up for their money. Perhaps a brief trip to England would do him good. He very seldom delivered himself but he would have admitted that his nerves were stretched and the outing would perhaps relax him. In which case he would take Russell's cash too, and of course he would have lunch at Mogg's. He had a passion for silverside, all the trimmings – carrots and onions and small sweet dumplings. In Holland they never got it quite right and it was one of Mogg's justified specialities.

He knew Russell's number and rang him up; he said in his slightly stilted English:

"A matter in which you were interested has come to a successful conclusion. I am coming to England shortly. Can we meet?"

"I'm at your disposal."

"Then perhaps you would lunch with me."

"Thank you. With pleasure."

"Would Thursday suit you?"

"Thursday – certainly."

"Then let us meet at Mogg's at a quarter to one."

Charles Russell was pleased for Mogg's was excellent. He didn't go there very often for it was beyond his own only moderate means, but he knew what he would order. Silverside.

The Prime Minister had read Laver's note with distaste, then thrown it into the shredder angrily. It was a waste of a busy man's time and he was one. He was holding his party together grimly lest it disintegrate under his eyes into ruin; he had a genuine hatred of all things to the Right but an equal contempt for the way-out Left. And now the rats were around his ankles, the men whom he nudged and backslapped in public, the Toms and Dicks and Harrys who wished him dead.

He was something more than busy; he was desperate.

And irritated by Richard Laver whom he had chosen to succeed Charles Russell, forcing the appointment through against opposition which had sometimes been vigorous. Richard Laver had been in the Cabinet Office, an able man and surely a sound one, but Alistair Leech was a good judge of character – he wouldn't have lasted a month if he hadn't been – and he had realised that Laver was also obsequious. Ambitious too – a good combination. Good for Mr Alistair Leech who wanted the blind obedience which Russell had occasionally withheld. But this paper was going too far; it was wasting time.

He rang Richard Laver up on the scrambler. He prided himself on his bluff sea-dog manner but there were people who thought him merely rude. "I got your note," he said. "Not helpful."

Richard Laver didn't like it. Besides, it was also grossly unfair. "Your standing orders – "

"I know about that. They were to keep an eye on Russell when abroad but not to report what is clearly irrelevant. I must ask you to use a greater discretion."

Richard Laver drew his breath in sharply for this wasn't the language of civil servants. It was in fact a reprimand and he wasn't accustomed to take them gracefully.

"I am sorry if I have erred," he said stiffly.

He had expected some emollient word but got none. The telephone in his hand was dead.

He was offended and the wound was raw since the assault had been both unfair and savage. And he'd had something else to pass on to Leech if the man had shown even moderate courtesy. He looked down at Willy Smith's report. Jane Lightwater had come up with something. Van Loons whom Russell had called on were being threatened.

He considered this but shook his head. It wasn't enough to restore his standing, for the counter-snub his ego craved.

No, but it was well worth a follow-up.

He wrote a message to his stringer in Holland, then sent it to Ciphers down in the basement. He expected there would be some delay since there'd been an outbreak of virulent influenza and the cipher room had been left shorthanded.

Willy Smith was not a cipher clerk but the Executive believed in all-round training and he had been taught the basic, essential techniques. On duty as a reluctant stand-in the message came down the tube to his desk. He was very far from being an expert but he knew that the secret was not to think. You simply took the words as they came and enciphered them without thinking of meaning. He did this and sent the message by telex, sending it to the stringer's office where his cover was a business in diamonds. The best sort of cover at that: it was genuine.

When he had done so but not before he read the words of the message for what they conveyed.

Am interested in movements of Karel van Loon, especially if he comes to England. In that case you are to mark him and report. His normal financial contacts are outside your scope but should he meet a Colonel Charles Russell you should report to me urgentest, if necessary on an open line.

William Wilberforce Smith absorbed this slowly. He looked at the clock; he had two hours to go. The stringer was prompt and mostly reliable, so with any luck he would see the answer before he was relieved of his watch.

It came to him with ten minutes to spare. It was in clear since it didn't need to be ciphered.

Message received and understood. Person referred to leaves Amsterdam Thursday Flight KL One-One-Five. Take off Zero Seven-thirty. Will accompany as instructed and contact.

. . . Jesus, he's after Russell seriously.

Willy Smith went home and lit a reefer. He didn't often smoke pot, he could take it or leave it. He knew there was a certain risk but he had very little taste for alcohol. Alcohol made you fat and soggy. Better a small accepted risk than a stomach you had to hold in with a body-belt.

He sucked in the smoke and exhaled it sensuously. It was extraordinary how it sharpened the mind. He had known that Laver detested Russell – well not exactly that; he was jealous. He was jealous of Russell's reputation and must know that he had opposed his appointment.

And now he was having Russell tagged. Just from envy? Unconvincing. No. It couldn't be that, or not alone.

Willy stabbed out the reefer for he had made up his mind. Charles Russell had appointed him, given him a job he liked, the sort of job which very few whites would have given to a man of his race. And he had treated him with scrupulous courtesy, more important with an unthinking equality. Willy was Russell's man till death freed him. He would have stood naked before his private conscience if he'd reneged on what he saw as his duty. Damn the Executive, damn Richard Laver.

But he realised that he was pushing his luck. He had once done something mildly irregular in telling Charles Russell he had been detailed to shadow him, but this was going to be more than irregular. He was going to tail Richard Laver's tail and he wasn't going to tell Richard Laver.

He looked at a time-table. Yes, seven-thirty. Seven-thirty from Schiphol and an hour for the flight. Time difference at the moment one hour.

Willy Smith would be at Heathrow on time though nature had loaded the dice against him. He wasn't cut out for the job of a shadow but he had done it before and would do it again.

Mogg's was an expensive restaurant patronised mainly by wealthy foreigners, Arabs and Japanese and West Germans. Charles Russell arrived in plenty of time and sat down in the foyer to wait for Van Loon. On the right was the girl who checked hats and umbrellas, in front of him a modern bar against mahogany which looked much older. A waiter came up and he ordered gin, to the head waiter he mentioned the name of Van Loon.

"Of course, sir. He has reserved a table."

"I haven't met him."

"I'll point you out to him."

Charles Russell sat quietly, sipping his gin. The foyer had begun to fill but he was confident that Van Loon would be punctual. At a quarter to one precisely he came in, speaking to the head waiter who nodded. Karel van Loon walked across to Russell.

"Colonel Charles Russell?"

Charles Russell stood up.

"I am Karel van Loon and delighted to meet you." They both sat down and Van Loon inquired: "Is that English gin you're drinking good?"

"Not outstanding and not the same as yours. But it's a reputable widely advertised brand."

"I understand. I'll take one too."

He gave the order to a passing waiter and on the table put a metal briefcase. It was about the size of a sheet of foolscap and maybe four inches in depth from the lid.

"The proceeds of Dame Molly's transaction. Since I was coming to London I brought it myself."

"She'll be more than grateful."

"It wasn't too difficult. There's a third in pounds, a third in guilders, but I had to bring the last third in dollars. I hope you don't object to dollars."

The irony was a trifle obvious but Charles Russell raised an appreciative smile. There'd been a time when men would kill for dollars but today they rated a mild apology.

"I don't mind at all – you can still manage to change them. And where can I return your briefcase?"

"Don't trouble – it's of little value. Compliments of the House of Van Loon.

They went into lunch and ordered quickly, the orders of men who'd already decided. An Arab had come in and was fussing, demanding the single table next to their own. It was clearly reserved but the Arab insisted. Money visibly passed and the Arab sat down. He spoke English but not with an Arab's accent.

Charles Russell said when they had eaten some silverside: "I was sorry to hear of your father's death."

"I shall miss him very much of course, but he was eighty-five and very frail and he'd lived a life which he never regretted."

Very smooth, Russell thought – entirely seemly. This man was slick – there was no other word. He was expensively dressed but not with elegance; he had spoken to the waiter crisply; he had ordered good wine but not an exciting one. He was the international business man making no attempt to be otherwise. Behind the politely impersonal manner would be a brain which reckoned in fractions of farthings.

"I imagine you will continue the business."

"To the best of my ability, certainly."

Again it was spoken with easy confidence but Charles Russell's antennae were long and sensitive. Something was being concealed but he couldn't guess what.

"With holidays at your house in Estoril?"

"You have heard of that?" It was suddenly sharp.

"When I last saw your father he mentioned it casually." Russell didn't go on but he remembered it clearly. The old man had meandered on ... "When I'm dead I expect he'll live there permanently." But that wasn't something to open up with a stranger who had just bought him luncheon.

Van Loon signed the bill and they rose together, and at the cloakroom the girl stopped Van Loon as he tipped her; she held an envelope out.

"Mister Karel van Loon?"

Van Loon took the note and looked at Russell. "Do you mind if I open it?"

"No, go ahead."

He opened it and went white as a handkerchief. Russell asked softly:

"Bad news?"

No answer.

There was a mirror behind the girl's head and shoulders and in it Russell had noticed movement. The Arab had turned in his seat and was watching them.

Van Loon had been very badly shaken.

"Are you all right?"

"Just give me a minute." Unexpectedly he held the message out. It was written in capitals cut from a newspaper.

DON'T THINK WE COULDN'T REACH YOU IN ENGLAND

Van Loon had recovered control with difficulty and Russell led him back to the foyer. He sat down but still shakily. Russell ordered brandy and Van Loon drank it. Some colour came back and Russell said:

"Has this happened before?"

"Yes, twice."

"In England?"

"The other two were in Amsterdam. That's what shook me – I mean that it happened here. The unexpectedness . . . Forgive me that scene."

The Arab had finished his lunch and had come to the foyer. He sat with a pot of coffee, impassive. He also had an air of alertness. Russell said suddenly:

"Spare a glance for that Arab. Have you seen him before?"

"Yes . . . No . . . I can't be certain. To tell you the truth they all look the same to me. But there was an Arab on my flight from Amsterdam."

Van Loon had been pulling himself together and Russell could risk a suggestion of action. "Do you think it's worth a word with that girl? She might remember who delivered that envelope."

Van Loon got up; he was now fairly steady. He returned and said quietly:

"She says the man spoke a pretty rough German."

"Significant?" Russell enquired.

"It could be. My father had a male nurse who spoke German. After my father died he disappeared."

"Then back to these threats. Do you know who is making them?"

Van Loon shook his head.

"So far only threats? No action?"

"Not so far."

41

"Demands for money?"

"No."

"That's interesting. I gather you're a wealthy man."

"I suppose you could say so."

"And it's happening all over the world. Kidnappings, holding to ransom, extortion."

"That's precisely what I'm afraid of – abduction. I think I'm being softened for the kill."

"Have you been to your police?"

"I haven't yet."

"I advise you to do so."

Charles Russell began to listen carefully. What he'd given had been classic advice but he knew that it wasn't always taken. Karel van Loon said:

"I'll go at once."

It had been firmly delivered, without hesitation, but Russell had caught the doubt behind it. He wasn't going to the police; he dare not. In the private cupboard of Karel van Loon was a large and probably malodorous skeleton.

Karel van Loon had got to his feet. "I'm sorry a pleasant luncheon was spoiled." He seemed normal again and Russell rose too. They collected their hats and umbrellas quietly and in the mirror Russell looked at the Arab. The Arab was still watching them closely.

The doorman rang a neighbouring taxi-rank. Van Loon asked:

"Can I drop you?"

"Yes please."

But in the street Russell suddenly changed his mind. "On second thoughts I think I'll walk. I'm putting on weight and I need the exercise." They shook hands and Karel van Loon drove away.

Charles Russell had told a social lie; he was neither putting on weight nor short of exercise but he had noticed something he hadn't expected. On the other side of the street, beyond the taxi, a man had been loitering, reading a newspaper. His hat was pulled well over his eyes, he wore a scarf and gloves though the day was warm. He had turned as Russell came through the door,

42

then started to walk away with his back to him. He walked well, with an athlete's easy stride.

Russell began to move too, but checked it. He wouldn't pursue and accost and humiliate. To do so with any West Indian was fatal, even with one as wholly anglicised as William Wilberforce Smith of the Security Executive.

But he would ring him up that evening and give him hell.

The Arab had shed his robes with relief and was sitting in front of Laver's desk. Richard Laver had been a civil servant and he liked to be sure that he had things right. "Run through it again," he said.

The stringer sighed; he thought he'd been clear enough the first time but if Laver wanted reassurance he could hardly flatly refuse to give it.

"So I found that Van Loon was coming to London. It was easy. He bought the ticket himself."

"So far so good."

"I then boarded the same flight as instructed."

"Did Van Loon recognise you?"

"I was dressed as an Arab."

"And then?"

"I tailed him from Heathrow to three banks. At each of them he left a package. Finally he went to Mogg's. Where, as you suggested he might, he made contact with Colonel Charles Russell openly."

"Did you hear what was said?"

"There was too much noise."

Richard Laver let this pass reluctantly. There were devices which greatly improved the hearing, particularly the directional hearing, but they were seldom issued to foreign stringers.

"After finishing lunch they went for their hats. The girl gave them an envelope and Van Loon opened it. I thought he was going to faint but he didn't. He showed the message to Russell and Russell looked grim. They went back to the foyer and Van Loon drank some brandy."

"And this time you heard a little?"

"Just snatches. Words like 'threats' and 'go to the police'. That was all."

The stringer had expected some praise but Laver found compliments hard to dispense. He nodded briefly.

"Keep me in touch, please."

When the stringer had gone Laver settled to think. It was something but it wasn't enough, not enough for what he badly wanted; he wanted to show Mr Alistair Leech that he wasn't the half-baked official he'd thought him. The assault had been grossly unfair in the first place but for that Richard Laver would make some allowances. Men under pressure were often testy and Leech was under mounting strain. But what he couldn't forgive had been Leech's manner. He, Richard Laver, a reasonably successful civil servant, had been treated like a defaulting clerk. His ego had been stripped and lashed; he would wake in the night and mutter uneasily as the enormity of the insult came back to him.

He knew that any thought of revenge would be a fantasy he had better not harbour and he certainly didn't expect an apology. Mr Leech had the ill-bred man's loathing of giving one. What he wanted was simply justification, the proof that he'd not only done his duty but done it with wisdom and proper judgment. Mr Leech might be bluff and rude and barbarous but he was a very long way from being stupid. He could recognise a counter-snub and the burr would stick and maybe fester.

Sir Richard Laver shook his head. What the stringer had told him might well be significant but it wasn't enough to take back to Leech. He ticked it off mentally. Van Loons were apparently being threatened which could easily be wholly irrelevant and Karel van Loon had come to London where he had contacted Charles Russell openly. That was interesting but proof of nothing. Russell had met him in Amsterdam and it was a very fair guess they had met to do business. So Van Loon comes to London to tie up the ends of it.

If he reported that to Alistair Leech he would earn himself another beating. He would have to wait till the cards were dealt him. Charles Russell might have done something questionable . . .

Now why was he always thinking of Russell?

44

4

The next day had been a heavy one and Van Loon chose to walk home through the Vondelpark. He had had threats before but not in London and he hadn't entirely recovered from shock. A brisk walk through the park might relax him finally. It was a beautiful evening, cool but clear.

There were lights in the old houses now and from one of them came laughter and music, discreet burgher music, discreet burgher laughter. He went into the park and sat down, admiring the play of the lights on the water. The ducks were squatting in huddles, asleep. Presently he began to walk again.

He had gone perhaps a hundred yards when the pistol came into the base of his spine. "Keep walking," a voice behind him said. It spoke Dutch but with a German accent. "And listen very carefully if you wish to continue unharmed till we're ready. Do anything foolish and you're going to get injured. That would only postpone what is going to happen and earn you a dose of avoidable suffering. Now don't look round and keep on walking."

The pressure on the spine was suddenly gone. Jan had slipped away in the shadows.

Karel van Loon reached his house and his study. He drank two brandies much faster than usual for now he was more shaken than ever. That was twice in thirty-six hours, twice too many.

So Jan *did* kill my father, he thought for an instant. But no, that was unproven still. For what would be advanced by killing him? Nothing. But the fact that Jan had disappeared had left the seed of doubt to nag and sap strength.

These people knew their business perfectly. They were keeping him on the rack without pity.

And it would have been useful to have an inside contact, one who had been entirely trusted. How much had he discovered and did it matter? Karel van Loon had indeed a skeleton but he was also twice a millionaire and all such men were nowadays vulnerable. They became more vulnerable every day as the framework of civilisation crumbled. Even in well conducted Holland they'd be a target for international operators. A snatch, he thought – duress, much pain.

He shivered and poured himself another brandy. He would now have to go to the police after all, and if the police knew what he feared they did, cooperation was by no means certain.

Charles Russell rang Willy Smith that evening; he was angry and making no effort to hide it. "What the devil are you playing at?"

"Sir?"

"Don't try a cover-up – I saw you outside Mogg's myself. And if there's one thing I detest it's lying."

"Lying?"

"You heard what I said. You told me on that aircraft once that I wasn't followed inside this country. Yet there you were in a horrible hat."

"With respect you have it just slightly wrong. I told you that the Executive wasn't interested in your movements in England."

"Then what were you doing at Mogg's?"

"I was on my own."

There was a silence before Charles Russell said mildly: "I think you had better come round and see me."

"May I come at once?"

"That's quite convenient."

Willy Smith arrived by taxi a half hour later. Russell had mellowed on a couple of whiskies and he poured Willy Smith a very small one. He knew that Willy Smith drank little and he was tolerant of the occasional reefer. But he didn't want a reefer here. The smell of marijuana made Russell sick.

Willy sat down and Charles Russell began on him. An excellent interrogator he didn't start by demanding answers; he preferred to let them come to him casually. "How's the cricket?" he asked.

46

"I don't get as much as I'd like or am used to. We've been terribly shorthanded lately."

William Wilberforce Smith was a passionate cricketer and also, in his class, a good one. He was that unfashionable animal, a leg-break bowler. He could roll his hand all day to a difficult length, he had a wrong-un without cocking his wrist too obviously, and a top spinner which fizzed off like a snake. He needed the right sort of wicket to bowl on but had once gone through Eton for ninety-eight. Now he played good class club cricket when he could.

"I'm sorry you don't get as much as you'd like."

"But I got a couple of days against the Greenjackets."

"How did you do?"

"Oh, not too badly."

"Come clean."

"I got six wickets."

"For what?"

"Seventy, as it happens."

"I see your hand hasn't lost its cunning but in your official life I think you've gone dotty."

"You're referring to my presence at Mogg's?"

"What else should I be referring to?"

Willy Smith sipped his tiny whisky, collecting his thoughts. "Do you remember a girl called Jane Lightwater?"

"Vividly. She's a high-class whore whom we paid to feed us. Very useful she was with all those diplomats. I took her on myself, I remember. She is also a rather distant cousin."

The words relaxed Willy Smith completely. So far he'd been understandably stiff but now he felt warm and contented; he felt 'in'. For this was the way the English did things and in all the world they had no rivals. There were countries with larger organisations, others with very much bigger budgets, but only one other had this effortless network and there it was a matter of race . . . You fee a tart to peach on diplomats and goddammit she's the boss's cousin! He was proud of the job which Charles Russell had given him and he wouldn't have changed it for any on earth.

Which made what he was doing riskier.

"She has had more than a whisper that Van Loon is in trouble. 'Threatened' was the word she used, so as likely as not someone's scaring his guts out as a preliminary to a straightforward snatch. There's a lot of it about, as you know."

"And what has this to do with me?"

"You went to Holland to call on Van Loon."

"I did and I can tell you why. Molly Pegg had some money stuck in Italy and I a wartime contact with old Van Loon. So I asked him to help and help he did, or more accurately after his death his son did."

"Do you know how the House of Van Loon makes its money?"

"I've heard more than one story but none is relevant. I don't have that sort of money or anything like it, and to the best of my knowledge nor has Dame Molly. What Karel van Loon got back out of Italy he handed over in notes at Mogg's." The manner of mild reasonableness changed. "Now tell me how you knew we were meeting there."

"I saw something I shouldn't."

"And used it?"

"I'm your man."

It came over with a complete simplicity. Charles Russell was touched but contrived to conceal it. "You're running an appalling risk."

"I'm ready to accept it."

"Why?"

"I suspect you're in danger but I don't know what danger yet. But Karel van Loon was tailed from Holland. I tailed the tail. He was dressed as an Arab and went to Mogg's after you. In fact he was our stringer in Amsterdam."

Charles Russell was outraged and said so. He'd heard rumours that the Executive had been slipping of late but he hadn't supposed it had reached rock bottom. Disguises were very old hat, amateurish, and amateurish was the worst word he knew. And in this case they were the mark of poor homework. This stringer would be unknown to Van Loon as he was certainly unknown to Russell; he could have walked into Mogg's in a city suit and neither would have been any the wiser. The Executive had gone down three classes. Disguises! He began to swear softly.

Willy sat quietly till anger abated. He admired these occasional outbursts of choler for they were one of the bonds which bound him to Russell. Russell treated him like a gentleman, which he had excellent reason to think he was, but more important he never gave special treatment, he never held back or minced his words because Willy's race was supposed to be touchy. When he was angry he tore a strip off. Willy liked it that way: it made him feel that he wasn't just hired. Richard Laver exuded consideration and William Wilberforce Smith resented it.

Russell had recovered urbanity. "Thank you for the information. Now I'll give you a bit in return for yours. Karel van Loon *is* being threatened – I assume, like you, as a step to extortion. When we went to get our hats and coats the attendant handed over an envelope. He opened it and it shook him badly. It was a warning he wouldn't be safe in England."

"Did the Arab see it?"

"I'm sure he didn't, but he did see something serious had happened. He was watching us in a mirror. I noticed it."

"Give me a minute to think it over." Willy took the full sixty seconds. "Now I'm surer than ever you're in very real danger."

"I must ask you from whom."

"And you know I cannot possibly tell you."

Charles Russell let this pass in silence, thinking that Willy Smith exaggerated. He knew that Laver didn't love him but he didn't believe it went further than that. But Willy was talking again and he listened.

"Will you be seeing Van Loon again?"

"I haven't any reason to – none. I'll be taking the money to Dame Molly tomorrow and I know how she intends to use some of it. She's going to blow it on a rather grand holiday. She has taken a villa in Estoril."

"Where Karel van Loon has a villa too."

Russell remembered the father mentioning it but was surprised that Willy Smith knew too. Willy saw it and said:

49

"We've a file on Van Loon on a different aspect. The money side."

"Ah yes, of course."

But it wasn't quite 'of course': it was curious. Russell put it aside since he couldn't evaluate it.

Willy was repeating his question. "So you won't be seeing Van Loon again?"

"I told you. I haven't a reason to do so."

"If you ever do, don't see him here."

It took a moment for the meaning to click. "You're suggesting I'm bugged but I very much doubt it. After I retired, you see, the Executive came round and checked."

"If they checked this flat they could also plant in it."

"Why should they do that?"

"I don't know. Suspicion, perhaps. Or over-insurance."

"Would you care to look around?"

"It wouldn't do any good if I did. On the box you see the famous operator going round a room with a gadget. When he hits the bug the gadget bleeps. But it hasn't been like that for some time. Most of the time a bug isn't activated so it doesn't respond to electronics. But you can activate it in several ways, when a listener ten miles away can hear as well as a man in your room."

"Horrible things."

"They've been greatly developed."

William Wilberforce Smith sat suddenly upright; he said with an unaccustomed emphasis:

"It's not what you do which causes trouble. It's what other people may think you're doing."

Charles Russell rose and held out his hand. "There's a corny old word but I'm not ashamed of it. The word is loyalty. You have it."

Commitment, he thought a little later, was a much more contemporary word.

He detested it.

5

Karel van Loon was a man of substance and had important people to smooth his path, so 'going to the police' had meant to the top. He was sitting before the Commissaris now. He was a man from Below the Rivers, a Catholic, and not so many years ago his appointment would have been quite unthinkable. He hid an unbending sense of duty behind a manner which was deceptively easy.

"You say you've had four threats in all, two while your father was still alive, one in London the day before yesterday, and the fourth in the Vondelpark last night?"

"That is so."

"The one last night was the first *physical* threat? And the man who had the gun last night was the man who had been your father's nurse?"

"I'm sure of that."

The Commissaris didn't like what he heard, the steadily increasing pressure, then the calculated dose of terror. He had experience of extortioners and this lot, whoever they were, were professionals.

He considered his own position dourly for he was caught in a policeman's nightmare, between the horns. He knew how the House of Van Loon made its money: it concealed the assets of wealthy men from the envy, hatred and malice of socialist states. The Commissaris didn't object to that, nor did his political masters. The management fees were very high and often the capital stuck in Holland. In any normal and straightforward case such a man could demand protection and get it.

But this wasn't a normal case – far from it. For Karel van Loon was not what he seemed. In the war he had collaborated and he had collaborated in the meanest way. Whilst his father had been keeping his head down the son had been selling men and women in hiding and the Gestapo had been paying him well. Partly they had paid in cash but Van Loon had had a taste for paintings and the Germans had looted plenty of those. Several famous ones had just disappeared, perhaps in Berlin's final holocaust. The Commissaris, a southern Catholic, had no especial fondness for runaways but it outraged him that this prosperous pig should have been selling his fellow citizens into slavery and too often worse. Nothing had been done at the time. After the war the legal officers had looked at the case but had shaken their heads. There had been evidence but not enough and there were plenty of cases which were open and shut. But the story was on more than one file and if it leaked there would be a resounding scandal. The Commissaris's masters would not like that. It wasn't policy to love all Germans but it was policy to forget the war. A good Dutchman, he loathed the idea of trouble.

But he showed nothing of his private feelings. "You are asking me for protection, sir?"

"I feel I am entitled to that." It was stiff and was intended to be so.

The Commissaris turned it. "I will do what I can but it isn't routine. Effective protection means constant surveillance, two men in eight-hour watches and their reliefs. And at the moment we are understaffed."

"No doubt I could make a contribution."

The Commissaris was deeply offended. So money could buy anything, could it? But he showed nothing of this as he went on smoothly. "Be assured that we'll do whatever we can." A thought struck him and he asked more sharply:

"May I take it you haven't hired private protection?"

"I thought of it but I turned it down."

The Commissaris was relieved and looked it. Nothing was worse in a civilised state than a private army at one man's orders. Slightly mollified he went on less formally.

"Have you any idea who these people are? Apart from your father's nurse, I mean."

"I have none."

"Had this nurse any special contacts?"

"Not that I know of – the man lived out. But his father originally came from Germany."

"And after *your* father's death he disappeared? You didn't see him again till that affair in the Vondelpark?"

"But it could have been he who brought that message in London."

The Commissaris considered it; he said at length on a note of apology: "I dislike the word gang, so we'll talk about groups."

"For a different reason I don't like it either. You're suggesting they're international terrorists?"

The Commissaris's solemn face permitted a smile. "There's a great deal of nonsense talked about terrorists. They exist, of course, they do form groups, and abduction is a speciality. But not all snatches are done by guerrillas. Some extortion rackets are run on business lines. Such a group has no political credo and the money to set up an operation doesn't come from some ill-intentioned Arab but from a business man who takes his cut when the operation turns out a success." The Commissaris looked at Van Loon and added: "Some respectable business man like yourself." He knew the remark was impermissible but Van Loon had offended by his offer of subsidy and his general air of 'I can buy it' was not to a good policeman's taste.

Van Loon had caught the faint note of irony but he let it pass since it was he who was suppliant. "Then you think that some non-political group – "

The Commissaris held his hand up at once. "No, I didn't say that – there isn't the evidence – but one such group is based in England and is financed and often even organised by a well-to-do British business man. Now the fact you received a threat in England is no sort of proof that it's those people after you but nevertheless I find it interesting."

Van Loon would have chosen a different adjective. "What do

you know of these people, then?" It came out roughly: Van Loon was scared.

"Little. Their main stamping ground is South America and they've never operated here in the Netherlands. Nor, for that matter, in England itself. I would guess that the British police know plenty, but if there hasn't been an offence in England and there aren't the hard facts for an extradition there is nothing they can do but keep watch." The voice changed again from speculation to business. "As I assure you we shall also do here. But I must make it plain I can guarantee nothing."

When Karel van Loon had taken his leave the Commissaris lit a cigar and frowned. Of the dangers he feared a big abduction came first. There had recently been a resounding state scandal but it had been smothered as only his nation could smother things, by simply pretending it wasn't there. But you couldn't do that with a major snatch; it would be fodder for all the Press of Holland and he himself in a hopeless position. He remembered what had happened before. In his view the only possible course had been to storm straight in and shoot it out, but no, they wouldn't wear that, they had parleyed for days. Pretty well everyone had got into the act, even a huddle of local psychiatrists, mumbling their incomprehensible jargon. The Commissaris had blushed and sweated; he had been shamed and he didn't wish it again, especially on behalf of Van Loon. He was a pig and a rogue but a millionaire, and in any part of the world that counted.

Especially in the sort of country which hotly denied that it counted at all.

Only one ray broke the policeman's gloom. He knew that Van Loon had a house in Portugal and he'd heard whispers that his future plans were to spend an increasing time at this villa. God send that the action was there, not in Holland. The Portuguese were a Latin people, less obsessed by the value of human life than were the humanist or Calvinist Dutch. They would go straight in and not much would come out. With any sort of luck at all Mijnheer Karel van Loon would not be one of them.

An unchristian thought? He was not feeling Christian; he was feeling that Van Loon had asked for it, and whoever now had

54

him hard on the rack might have more than the single motive of money. Did these extortioners know what he'd done in the war? To the Commissaris it began to look possible. A build-up of terror before the snatch was common where there weren't rich relations, where the abducted would have to be squeezed directly, but this one had been protracted unusually. Van Loon was already in serious trouble but any element of revenge would double it.

Van Loon went to his office with his feathers much ruffled. He couldn't deny he'd been treated with courtesy, but he hadn't expected so cool a detachment. And behind that detachment had lurked – well, what? Probably dislike. What of it? But there had also been the hint of knowledge and knowledge in this world was power.

And the Commissaris had also frightened Van Loon; he hadn't been openly cooperative but nor had he been reassuring, and he'd declined in terms to guarantee safety. England, Van Loon remembered suddenly. It was possible they operated from England.

A thought formed slowly but grew in the forming. He'd found a note from his father to do Charles Russell a service. The sum had been trifling, the commission nil, and Van Loon had considered discreetly defaulting. Now he was very glad he had not. For you never knew with a man like Russell when someday, somewhere, he couldn't be useful.

Karel van Loon rang Charles Russell in London. "May I come and see you? Urgently."

Russell was not ashamed to be taken aback. He had passed the money to Molly Pegg and been rewarded by an invitation to spend part of the summer in Estoril. Perhaps he would go and perhaps he wouldn't but the last thing he wanted was complication.

"Something has gone wrong?" he asked cautiously.

"About that money? Certainly not."

"Then if I may ask – "

"A personal matter I haven't yet mentioned."

Charles Russell was trapped and resented it bitterly. He hadn't much cared for Karel van Loon. He'd been polite enough but there'd been something about him, a faint but perceptible whiff of corruption. But he had done Charles Russell a considerable favour; he couldn't with decency just be brushed off.

"If you could give me some idea – "

"Not on the telephone."

Charles Russell conceded since he couldn't do otherwise; he sighed but he simply said: "When will suit you?"

"This evening. This evening at half-past six."

... By God, he's a thruster. Or else he's in really serious trouble.

"This evening at half-past six. Very well."

Russell poured a drink and over it thought. William Wilberforce Smith had asked him twice if he intended to see Van Loon again and after that had been decidedly Delphic ... "It's not what you do which causes trouble, it's what other people may think you're doing."

And here was Van Loon with urgent business. It was probably some quid pro quo and refusal wasn't going to be easy.

Laver's stringer was on an open line for he didn't have time for codes or ciphers. "It's urgent," he said. "I had to reach you."

"If it really is. But don't use names."

The stringer was offended deeply. He might not be quite a first-class man but he did know the basic rules and observed them. Just like Laver, he thought, to put a great foot in it. But he hid his rancour and went on deliberately.

"The individual in whom you are interested is returning to London this afternoon." He gave the flight number and ETA. "He has an appointment at half-past six precisely."

"With whom?"

"With Colonel Charles Russell at Russell's flat."

"You are sure of this?"

"I am prefectly sure."

"How are you sure?"

Again the offence but again the soft answer. "Van Loon has many enemies here and I have a contact in his private office. She's a woman and she hates his guts. It was something to do with her parents in the war."

Laver found it hard to commend but he managed a faintly grudging: "You've done well."

"I'll be following on the same aircraft myself."

"No."

"Did I hear that correctly?"

"Yes, you did. This time we know where he's going and when. That's enough. We can handle this end ourselves without help."

The stringer was disappointed but rang off.

Richard Laver lit a cigarette. The action was entirely reflex. He couldn't use a telephone without a cigarette in the other hand. Now he picked up one of several on his desk.

"Masters?"

"Speaking."

"I'd like you to come down at once. And bring the log with you."

"Understood."

He was shown into Laver's room and asked to sit. Laver said: "Colonel Charles Russell." He gave an address.

Masters checked in his book, said loudly: "Affirmative." He had been watching American space films and unknowingly had caught the patter.

"You are confirming that the flat is planted?"

"I am doing just that."

"How long ago?"

Another look at the book. "When Russell retired – say five or six years ago."

"Will it still be working?"

"I don't see why not. It hasn't been checked since there wasn't the need to but I would bet that it could still be activated."

"I want that done at a quarter-past six."

"Tonight?" Masters looked at his watch. "It's pretty short notice."

"It's also important. And I intend to listen myself besides taking a tape."

"I'll make the arrangements. Anything else?"

"No, I think that's all."

Sir Richard Laver didn't say 'Thank you'.

And at six-fifteen he went up to the attic. He sat in a leather chair and waited, facing a bank of lighted instruments. An amplifier was on a separate table and somebody had remembered an ashtray. Two of the dials on the bank showed readings but the amplifier was coldly silent.

At six-thirty precisely two lights flashed red. A tape began to turn deliberately. The amplifier hummed, then said:

"Good evening Mijnheer Van Loon."

"Good evening."

"Good evening, Mijnheer Van Loon."

"Good evening."

Russell showed him to a chair. He had a glass in his hand and asked Van Loon:

"Would you care for a drink? I'm sorry I have no Netherlands gin."

"Whisky will do perfectly, thank you."

They were being a little formal on both sides, neither man ready to start the ball rolling. They talked indifferently of indifferent matters, the English weather, Van Loon's flight from Holland. It was Russell who asked finally:

"How can I help you?"

"My life is being threatened by some organisation I do not know."

"I remember you showed me a message at Mogg's."

"There were two others before the one at Mogg's and I've since had a gun in my back in a physical threat."

Charles Russell nodded but didn't speak. It sounded alarmingly expert and organised, the build-up of pressure, the knife turned pitilessly. Van Loon said at length:

"I want you to work for me."

Russell had suspected it for the request had been made before more than once. But it had never before been made by a man he mistrusted. And he owed this man an obligation. He would have to be more than usually careful.

"If any advice I can give – "

"I need more."

"I doubt if I could give it. How could I?"

"Will you listen to what I know?"

"I will."

"Then I've been to my own police by now, and I found them less than wholly cooperative." (Perhaps you have something to hide – it wouldn't surprise.) "But they did tell me something I didn't know. I knew that extortion was internationally organised and I'd believed that it was politically motivated. What I didn't know was that sometimes it isn't."

"That I can believe."

"So far so good. Forgive the word gangs but one constantly hears it. They have hyphenated names and give themselves airs; they're mostly anarchist with Arab money behind them. But one doesn't so often hear of extortion run as a straightforward business."

That's untrue, Russell thought, but he didn't say so.

"And one such organisation works from England. I can't be sure it's the one which is after me but if it is I need your help badly."

"You grossly overrate my competence. I haven't a machine behind me and in any case – "

"I'm a very rich man."

Not tactfully done, Russell thought – the straight buy. He was irritated but kept his temper, suddenly at his most urbane and lucid.

"I concede what you say could be true, but apart from that threatening letter at Mogg's this organisation, if indeed it exists, has done nothing to break English law and it's hardly likely to snatch you in England. In Holland I couldn't possibly help." He was tempted to add but decided not to: "Even if I wished to do so."

"I wasn't thinking of active protection. As you say, they're unlikely to kidnap me here. I was thinking that you might somehow frustrate them."

"How?" Russell asked. He was getting bored. In its way such a proposition was flattering but he had had it too often and was merely annoyed.

"I should naturally leave the mechanics to you."

"And you would leave them without the least hope of success. I must make my position clear and final. If these people commit any crime in England that's a matter for the English police."

"I can't persuade you to change your mind?"

"I'm very much afraid you cannot."

Van Loon rose to go but Russell stopped him. He was conscious that he hadn't been gracious and he owed this man a considerable favour. "But though there's nothing I can do I can still give advice. That is, if you think it worth the taking."

Van Loon sat down at once. "I do."

"I believe you have a villa in Portugal. I know because your father mentioned it. If I were in your shoes I'd go and stay in it."

"I must admit I have had the same idea."

"There would be more than one advantage in that. In the first place, if I'm understanding you rightly, your own police felt unable to give you exactly whatever it was you were asking for. The Portuguese police might be more cooperative." Russell added without a muscle moving: "After all, as you said, you're a very rich man."

It was a reproof but Van Loon, who was Dutch, either let it pass or didn't notice it.

"I had already considered that," he said.

And done rather more than just consider. That thug in the gatehouse, the strongroom they were making the cellar, the grilled windows and the electric fence . . .

"And then there's the question of foreign countries – I mean of violence outside your own. All these kidnappers have their own special stamping grounds, the North Europeans in Northern Europe, the Italians almost wholly in Italy and the Arabs all over the Middle East. I assure you it's very hard indeed to operate in a strange environment. You don't know the language, you haven't the contacts. I am speaking from a real experience. An England-based group might snatch you in Holland especially with a Dutchman in it but I'll lay a good deal of hard-earned money that it wouldn't have a chance in Portugal, or not without total re-organisation. And if, as you say, they are run as a business that might show them a thumping minus return."

"You're saying it's going to be Holland or nowhere?"

"More or less."

"How more and how less?"

"That would be my private bet."

Van Loon rose for the second time. "I'm disappointed," he said, "but also grateful."

"Advice costs nothing."

"But can sometimes be useful."

When Van Loon had left Russell poured more whisky. He had noticed the other's empty glass but hadn't felt inclined to refill it. Now he filled his own and sat down, scowling.

> *The reason why I cannot tell*
> *I do not like you Doctor Fell*

Richard Laver had played the tape back twice. He sat in an official's heaven, the knowledge he had been right and could prove it. The Prime Minister wouldn't apologise – Sir Richard Laver did not expect it – but underneath that sea-dog manner was a certain if limited sensibility which would hardly fail to notice a snub. For Mr Alistair Leech was being diminished. Richard Laver had obeyed an order, possibly an otiose order, and all he had got for his pains had been censure; he'd been rebuked like an inefficient underling. But now he had been proved right. It was good.

He took paper and began to write again: *The Rt Hon Alistair Leech, P.C., M.P.*

He looked at this rubric and smiled at it acidly. He would never be a Privy Councillor but he thought himself brighter than Alistair Leech.

He wrote in his graveyard Mandarin English, never stating more than he knew nor less … As the Prime Minister would already know Charles Russell had seen *père* Van Loon in Amsterdam. In view of their previous wartime contact that visit might well be entirely innocent but subsequent developments might lead (he didn't say they formally did) to a conclusion of a different nature. For young Van Loon had twice come to England and on each occasion had made contact with Russell. On the first, when they had met at a restaurant, Van Loon had been seen to be handed a message and that message had visibly shaken him badly. The second had been at Russell's own flat where what passed had been put on tape –

He crossed this out and wrote instead: where what passed had been duly recorded. He had learnt a good deal as an Under Secretary.

– and the burden of this conversation had been, at the very lowest, interesting. Van Loon had begun with a clear admission that he himself was being threatened, adding, though with less than certainty, the belief that the extortioners were operating from England. He had sought Russell's help and had offered to pay for it, but Russell had turned that down unequivocally. He had, on the other hand, offered advice, and the nature of that advice had been curious. *It was more curious, perhaps, that it was offered at all if his contacts with Karel van Loon were innocent.* The advice to Van Loon was to go into hiding, in Portugal where he owned a villa.

We shall continue to pursue this matter and will welcome any specific instructions.

(So Ya! to you Mr barbarous Leech.)

Laver sent this letter by hand again and rang for a cup of strong black coffee. Leech could put that in his pipe and smoke it, and if the taste was sour he had certainly asked for it. The coffee increased Laver's quiet euphoria. He had heard of hubris but had seldom considered it. In fact he'd been marked as the old gods' victim. Though he didn't have any idea he had done so, this intelligent, conscientious official had jumped from the ordered world of Security into the roaring furnace of party politics.

6

What Laver had hoped for from Alistair Leech was the gentle nod of recognition: this was competent work, the man wasn't a fool. Laver hadn't expected praise or thanks since Alistair Leech wasn't given to either, but equally the last thing he'd thought of was that Leech would be thrown into private panic.

For Mr Alistair Leech, a party moderate, had eight hundred thousand pounds with the House of Van Loon. It was all of it in bearer bonds, he was brought the income twice yearly in cash, and on it he paid no tax in England. Since he and Phyllis his wife were childless the arrangement suited them very well.

It suited them very well indeed so long as the fact of it stayed a secret.

He shuddered at what would happen if it did not. His left wing was already after his blood and at Conferences mauled him severely; his Cabinet, he knew, was bored with him; he was a superlative wheeler-dealer, a fixer, and since he lacked established principles would compromise till the stitching parted. There was also nobody else whom the centre would trust. But there were limits to reluctant loyalty and one of them would be tax evasion on a scale which wouldn't shame a duke. And it wouldn't be only political rivals who would tear his shrinking carcase to pieces. The whole of the party's ethos would be outraged. It still had deep roots in the anti-establishment and deeper still in nonconformity. Neither would stand for this; they'd revolt. He could easily lose the next election and, to Alistair Leech much more important, his own career would be finished finally. He wouldn't be Prime Minister and he could easily lose his own safe seat.

Moreover it couldn't be stopped at that, the scandal of a progressive Prime Minister behaving like a hated capitalist. Inevitably there would be an enquiry, they would question and probe, they would burrow like moles, till they discovered how he had made his money. Honestly, he himself considered, but it was very unlikely that everyone else would. Some of it had come from Phyllis but a great deal he'd earned and saved himself. In opposition he'd been a successful journalist and had written a book which had sold well in America, but the principles upon which he'd invested offended everything which his party stood for . . . Would this investment increase employment? Then no sensible man would even consider it. Either it would go quietly bankrupt and be nationalised, your shares near worthless, or if it made profits and somehow stayed public, the Unions would squeeze it remorselessly. WAGES BEFORE PROFITS – he had seen that banner. But if a business were safely labour-intensive, merchant banking, say, or developing property, the sensible man couldn't get in fast enough. Leech had had a proven system; he had given his broker political guidelines and his broker had translated these into purchases which had been wildly successful.

Successful, yes, but also offensive. Offensive to all progressive thought. To hell with progressive thought. Let it rot.

Unhappily he would sink without it.

He did what he always did in a crisis, talking to his wife for advice. As he knocked on her door the masseuse came out of it. Phyllis was on her bed, stark naked. She had faded a little but not very much and she still had a magnificent body. She didn't bother to pull a sheet up. It was a deliberate insult: her husband knew it. He looked at her and nothing stirred.

He handed her the note from Laver and she sat up in bed and reached for her spectacles. Both arms went up where one would have served her and for a moment she held the model's pose tauntingly. Then: "Bring me my dressing gown, please."

He brought it.

She put it on and her glasses too, reading Richard Laver's message. At the end she said simply: "You're in the shit." She spoke an upper-class doric which often offended him but she seldom failed to make clear her meaning.

"You think there's some mischief brewing?"

"What else?"

"Richard Laver doesn't quite say that."

"Richard Laver's a civil servant, a twit. Richard Laver wouldn't quite say anything without a sheaf of affidavits to back him." She noticed that he had begun to sweat for the bedroom was kept at a steady eighty. Phyllis Leech loved three things before all others; she loved sun and good food and experienced lovers.

Her husband Alistair gave her the food.

"That money – " he began again.

She made a gesture of contemptuous despair. "You needn't go all through that – I know it. If that came out you'd be finished politically. The Lefties would tear you to pieces and love it."

"The party too."

"The party," she said, "can go and play pouffes." She changed gear with a corrosive illogic. "What motive would Russell have for poking about?" She had known him once and for a time hotly fancied him but at that moment he'd been engaged with another and the other woman had been her friend. She was a ruthless and wholly amoral woman but one thing she was not was a thief. She asked again: "What motive could Russell have?"

"I don't know that."

"Then I suggest you think." Characteristically she did it for him. "You sacked him, didn't you?"

"No, not at all. He just went when his contract expired, that's all."

"But he could have had an extension?"

"Probably."

"Did he ask for one?"

"No."

"I bet he didn't. Did you offer one?"

"No, of course not."

"Why 'of course'?" She looked at his fleshy sexless face; he was going to go into his statesman act and of all things she hated she hated that most. He said with a measured deliberation:

"The Left was somewhat hostile to Russell."

She managed to suppress her laughter which on another occa-

65

sion she would have released uninhibitedly. But at this moment she had another question and laughter dried up Alistair helplessly.

"He didn't get any honour, did he?"

"I don't think he's the sort to care for them."

She thought this assumption excessively dangerous, the sort of self-deception her husband loved. If you happened to be making it wrongly then you also made a bitter enemy without even the knowledge of having done so.

"Give me a cigarette," she said. She knew he didn't smoke but carried them and he gave her one from a gold cigarette case. She had given it him when her father died and the gift had been as Greek as they came. It was in high carat gold, Edwardianly vulgar, and inside was engraved a crest and a coronet. She had known he could never use it in public: it wouldn't go down with the brothers and sisters. But he carried it still and she thought she knew why.

He fumbled in his coat for his lighter but she lit the cigarette herself. She would try to forget him, he inhibited thought. He had plenty of conditioned reflexes, the sort which had served him well in politics, but he couldn't think clearly outside his coordinates.

She had come a long way to nowhere but the choice had been hers. She had spotted him as a rising young man and she'd been crazy for a life in politics. Real politics, power, not the charade which was smothering her.

It was curious how the genes reverted; she was back to her grandfather, even to his father, and both had been as tough as army boots. They had been steelmasters in a Midland town who had sweated their way from nothing to wealth. Her grandfather had bought an estate though he'd heartily despised his neighbours, and then, as she knew had happened often, the drive had slipped for a generation. The third had been ripe for the higher thought and her father had swum in the sewage happily. He'd been high-minded, earnest, intelligent, futile; he'd been a Liberal Whip and had earned his peerage but Phyllis's childhood had not been happy. She had liked the fine old house in Highgate but the people who had frequented it, no. Even now they could make her sweat in shame, the latest socially conscious novelist, the teachers with ample private means who felt it a duty to teach in Africa, the preposterous broken-down Indian holy-men, the whole ragbag of a world she despised. What she had longed for was active politics, the hard rough and tumble of power and advancement. She had made no choice between Left and Right: either would serve her purpose equally and Leech had been a coming man.

Now he was Prime Minister and asking her what to do in a crisis.

"Eight hundred thousand pounds," she said, "and in passing quite a bit of it mine."

"We'd have my pension."

"Your pension is piddle."

"It was you," he said, "who suggested Van Loons."

... So now it's The Woman Tempted Me, is it? For once she concealed her contempt successfully, but she looked at him as her grandfather might have, conscious of his abilities, the power to subvert and fix and compromise, but unwilling to give him the meanest job.

But he had started again. "Do you think that Russell – ?"

"Do I think he's playing some game with Van Loon? Something which might bounce back on us even if we're not the first target?" She nodded emphatically. "Yes, I do. He can reasonably feel he's been shabbily treated. I don't suppose he minded too much that he didn't get some wretched honour but it was the way you simply dropped him that must have hurt. To suppose that men forget these things is the action of a very great fool."

"Then what sort of game is Russell playing?"

"I don't know that and I don't pretend to. But Russell is the great unknown and great unknowns are always dangerous."

"Then what do we do?"

"Simplify the equation, my husband. Eliminate Russell and see what happens."

For a moment he didn't connect with her meaning, but when he did he stood up stiffly.

"Sit down, you fool, and listen to me. Doesn't Laver have an organisation? Doesn't he have to do as you say?"

"Both statements are entirely correct." He was back on his statesman manner again.

"Then have him up and tell the whole story."

He was utterly astonished. "But – "

His wife interrupted with a dangerous patience. "Can't you see that's the only hold you have on him? To make him do as you wish, I mean."

"No, I don't see that."

"Then I'll try to explain. How long has Laver to go on secondment?"

"Three or four months."

"Then there you are. If this story breaks you're no longer Prime Minister. Either a Leftie will push you out or there could even be a general election. In neither case would Laver last long. You say that the Left didn't care for Russell but the way-out Left loathes Laver too. Occasionally he does his job – that communist miner, for instance. That shook them. And if an election went the wrong way and you lost it Laver wouldn't last a week. The Right thinks he's soft and in their sense he is. They'd out him and he surely knows it. There you are," she concluded, "a gert great stick. A change from the usual diet of carrots."

He rose at last. "I'll think it over."

"You bloody do that or we've both of us had it."

When he had gone she nodded, satisfied. She knew he would summon Laver – he'd have to. It would be hard on Charles Russell whom once she had fancied, but he wasn't as young as once he had been and he was the sort who would prefer a bullet to dying in some institution.

She wondered how that ass her husband would handle the little chat with Laver, which of his manners he'd feel was appropriate. He had four of them and he rang the changes. The first was a repetitive rhetoric which went down well at annual Conferences, the second the bluff sea-dog style which he used with beer and curling sandwiches before the Trade Union barons wiped their boots on him. The third was a sort of matey wheedle and the fourth was openly bluster, bullying. She nodded again for she'd

68

made up her mind. With Laver it would be simply bullying, and being the half-man he was he'd give in.

She looked at her diary. It was not a good evening. They were dining the Attorney General. He was a greying hack and of little importance, but once a year they had to have him. His forte was explaining the inexplicable, how Trades Union law, the law on picketing, was really perfectly clear and simple. Anybody who tinkered was mad. Later he would drink too much if Alistair Leech could not forfend it. He was utterly without charm or graces.

She had the gift of instant sleep and now used it; she never took drugs since she didn't need them. It was going to be a grisly evening so she might as well snatch an hour's quiet nap. The affair of Charles Russell she had put out of her mind. That was another gift and a big one. There was nothing she could do to help till her husband and Laver had had it out and she didn't believe that Laver would stand. Then why worry? An hour's sleep was better.

As she dropped off she grunted happily. It was going to be a horrible evening but tomorrow she was seeing John. John had taught her nothing new but he did what he did with a vigorous competence.

7

The red telephone rang on Laver's desk and a voice said pleasantly:

"Good morning, Sir Richard."

"Good morning, Prime Minister."

Laver was more than surprised, he was wary. Leech seldom called Richard Laver 'Sir Richard'. His impression, suppressed with resentment, was that if Alistair Leech had been a Latin and Laver only a few years younger Leech would have used the Second Singular.

"I'd be grateful if you could come and see me."

... 'I'd be grateful' – that was most unusual.

"I'm at Chequers so I'll send a car. Say in about an hour and a half."

Laver rearranged his engagements. It was desk-work and he did it well, for he knew all the drills and applied them smoothly, the excuse to one man, the truth to another.

At a quarter-past twelve the big car stopped finally. The journey had been slow and frustrating and Laver who'd been edgy on starting was now very close to apprehension. He went up the steps of the ugly old mansion and was shown into the Prime Minister's study.

"Very kind of you to come so suddenly. Naturally the matter is urgent. Will you have a drink?"

"Thank you. Black coffee."

They sat down in armchairs beside the fireplace, informal and deliberately matey. Laver, who wasn't dull-witted, tautened. He didn't like the smell of this, not after Leech's recent discourtesy.

"I read your last note with the greatest interest. Charles Russell is playing a dangerous game."

"Not yet an altogether clear one, but as I said we'll continue to watch and report."

"I'm afraid I cannot accept that position." The tone had changed and Laver noticed it. "We're assuming there'll be another development and that development may well throw more light. But it may also prove entirely disastrous."

"Disastrous to whom?"

"To me."

Laver who was experienced waited. The Prime Minister straightened his back in his chair.

"I have eight hundred thousand pounds with Van Loons."

It hit like an armoured division, brutally. Leech noticed the impact and welcomed it warmly. Laver had seen the implications. It wouldn't have pleased him to have to spell them out.

"Will you have another coffee?"

"Yes, please."

Alistair Leech rang the bell for the coffee. Laver noticed he wasn't drinking himself.

"I think we'd do well to eliminate Russell."

"Eliminate?"

"I said 'eliminate'. My wife put it rather neatly, I thought. She saw it as a sort of equation where one of the terms is unknown and variable. Remove that unknown and the solution is simple."

... Of course he would go to his wife and pick her brains. One couldn't describe the man as uxorious but subservient he certainly was.

"And how does one eliminate Russell?"

"I must leave that to you – after all it's your business."

"I doubt that seriously."

The manner changed at once to the bullying. "Doubt by all means but do as I say. After all it's been done before more than once. Russell himself did it several times."

The back-reference to Charles Russell stung for it confirmed what Laver had long suspected, that though Leech had been forced to let Russell go he would have preferred him as a partner in business. He put down his cup and said deliberately:

"And if I decline?"

"You will not decline." The manner now wasn't merely a bully's, it was a very unpleasant bully's indeed. "You will not decline because you dare not. Either Right of me or further Left you woudn't last a week and you know it. You're in this as deep as I am or deeper."

"I'll think it over," Laver said.

"Do that if you find it helps you. But the sooner you show some action the better."

Laver went out to the waiting car; he was trembling but not with fear. They seemed to be taking a different route and he asked the driver:

"Making a detour?"

"Not for Slough station, sir."

"The station?"

"Those were my orders – to take you to Slough."

So the knife had begun to turn already.

In his office he ordered his third black coffee. It was two above his normal ration, but a stopping train hadn't soothed his nerves nor a journey with an insolent taxi-man. He knew that time was now against him and his training had taught him the value of time.

For what that odious man had said had been true: Richard Laver was nailed to his private cross. In his profession he'd been an Under Secretary, a rank well above the level of competence, but he had begun to suspect that there he would stick. The days of the great magic circle were over, the Wykehamist scholars, the Balliol Firsts. You still needed academic excellence if you were to make the First Division at all but the men at the top now had more than that; they had to have more than that to survive. In his own boss he had sensed a certain reserve and could guess what he'd say to another real bigwig. There was an accepted civil service jargon ... "Laver? Oh yes, very able indeed, but he does have certain defects of character."

So he'd been delighted when unexpectedly they had offered him the Security Executive. Formally it had not been promotion, for though there was a generous allowance he was to keep his existing and substantive rank. In a sense he'd been shunted but the siding was cosy. And out of the formal ladder of precedence an honour had been well within reach. Laver who knew these ropes had used them. After that he had had it worked out precisely. An extension in the Security Executive, and then, still in his fifties and notably knighted, the directorship in some well-known company, ostensibly something to do with Security. The Is were all dotted, the last T crossed.

And now if he lost his job he was finished. He would still have his substantive rank – it meant nothing. He couldn't go back to the civil service, a knighted Under Secretary, a failure. They would shunt him again and this time less pleasantly. And in the stuffy clubs which the top men frequented they would smile when they mentioned Sir Richard's name. Somehow he had to keep his job.

He had been born in a High Anglican vicarage and had been trained to make the worse seem the better case. This conditioning now seized him powerfully. In the height of its glory or maybe shame (which depended on your political ethos) the Executive had been sometimes ruthless, but any action would have been out of the question unless Russell himself had given the order. So Russell was himself a killer . . .

Laver shook his head. That wouldn't do. Those men who had mostly discreetly vanished had been enemies of the state and endangering it. There'd been commendably elastic rules about that. But was Russell endangering the state? He was not. He was endangering Mr Alistair Leech and with him his creature, Sir Richard Laver. Who didn't care for the word but was obliged to accept it. If Leech fell in some enormous scandal Richard Laver would surely choke in its dust.

He tried another tack more hopefully. Leech, after all, had said 'eliminate': the dread word 'kill' had not been uttered. But again he shook his head reluctantly. His talent for self-deception was high but he had known very well what Leech had meant. Besides, there was the practical side. Persuade Russell to go abroad for a year, then quote to Leech the word 'eliminate'?

Leech would probably sack him on the spot. It was a sound enough point in the world of semantics but semantics were not the Prime Minister's strong point.

And another doubt troubled a well-trained conscience. Men had been known to kill in anger: there were even countries with special laws for it. But he wouldn't be killing in honest anger, he'd be killing to save the political skin of a man whom he detested wholeheartedly and with it his own material future. He couldn't tell himself that he hated Russell, only that he was resentful and envious. Of Russell's panache and cool detachment, the way he made everything look so easy. Perhaps, he thought, if I hated Russell, if he'd humiliated me as Alistair Leech has . . .

He had risen quite high in his own profession which meant he was an experienced staller. Postponing action was called good judgment. Never do a thing until forced to.

He picked up a telephone and rang Charles Russell; he would be grateful if Russell would come and talk to him.

An ironical echo mocked his words. 'I'd be grateful,' Alistair Leech had said before he'd reached for the bludgeon and battered down Laver.

He wished passionately he had private means, enough to spit in Leech's eye. As Russell had had.

To hell with Russell.

Charles Russell looked round the familiar room. It had changed from his own time to insignificance. The two old Persian rugs were gone and the Roberts' Spanish Scenes from the walls. In his own flat Russell had room for neither and had given them to a favourite niece. The battered but rather fine old boards were covered with carpeting wall to wall, and there was an abstract from the Offices Pool which no doubt conveyed some esoteric message. Russell sat in a repro Chippendale chair, opposite Laver, the desk between them. If their positions had been reversed, he was thinking, he would have sent for a second armchair and talked comfortably.

Laver in turn was watching Russell, the well-made, faintly Edwardian suit, the tie with its tidy, unfashionable knot, the old but once expensive shoes, meticulously kept and polished. Russell's hat hung on the bent-wood hatstand and Laver had noticed the lining was spotless. It had reminded him that his own needed cleaning.

Richard Laver had decided his line; he was going to use shock tactics and watch the effect. "I think you're in very great danger," he said.

"Then of course I shall expect your protection."

It wasn't the expected answer and it threw Richard Laver neck and crop. For after Charles Russell's discreet retirement the Executive had, for some months, kept an eye on him. There had been men who might reasonably seek revenge and Russell's death would be banner headlines, the sort of scandal a good civil servant detested. So there'd been a button on Russell's radio but pressing it hadn't produced a programme. It had produced an urgent call elsewhere on the desk of an alert duty officer. But as time went by and nothing happened the watch had been relaxed, then abandoned. The very last thing Richard Laver wanted was to be obliged to put it on again.

He looked at Russell, urbane and upright, thinking he hadn't lost his skills. "I'm afraid we couldn't do that," he said. He realised that it sounded feeble.

"You mean that you have no authority."

Laver had expected questions, "What danger?", "From whom?" and "When and where?" The counter attack threw him flat on his face; he groped for some recovery, said:

"I'm sorry but I am perfectly serious." It sounded feebler than ever and Laver knew it.

"I didn't think you had asked me here to jest." There was a smile with this but not a wide one. Russell was still alert and wary but one of the questions expected came. "If you cannot protect me I must look after myself. In which case I must know what danger."

"It arises from your associations."

"All of them are now respectable."

For a moment Laver was off the hook but he suspected the

moment would not last long; he would use it while he could and said:

"You know Mr Karel van Loon?"

"I have met him."

"Do you know what he does?"

"I strongly suspect it. As far as I know he does nothing criminal, or nothing under Netherlands law, but to all men of the Left his trade is offensive. But I'm in no way concerned with Van Loon's profession. I'm not in the class which would even tempt him."

"Yet you met him twice."

"How do you know?"

Laver said quietly: "We had him tailed."

"Then clearly you have an active interest."

"If we hadn't I wouldn't have asked you to come here."

Charles Russell had a long experience and could play this sort of hand in his sleep. Laver had been doing the leading: now it was time Russell offered an opening. Laver might lead into strength or make a slip.

"I take it you still employ Willy Smith?"

Laver looked surprised but nodded.

"I was talking to him a few days ago and no doubt he reported back to you."

"Since then there has been a second visit. We shadowed Van Loon to your flat. He went in." A pause but slightly overplayed. "It would be helpful if you told me what happened."

"He made me a proposition. I turned it down."

"But you also gave him some free advice."

There was a total and astonished silence. Russell had been expecting some slip but hardly a resounding clanger. Evidently they had bugged his flat, an action he resented bitterly, much more for the manner than for what had been done. He had used bugs himself and despised hypocrisy but he had never bugged his immediate predecessor. Besides, the act had been wholly unnecessary. They had only to come and ask his permission and they could have bugged every room in Charles Russell's flat . . . Stringers disguised in Arab robes, and now an even worse offence, deviousness where none had been necessary. It confirmed an impression he had been forming reluctantly. The Executive had gone downhill badly.

None of this showed on his graven face for he could see that Laver had realised his blunder. He began to recapitulate, forcing Laver to make his discards hurriedly.

"So the position is that you think I'm in danger."

"I'm perfectly sure you're in very great danger."

"From which you will not protect me."

"I cannot."

"I understand your position perfectly but I cannot protect myself without knowledge." He sat suddenly bolt upright, formidable. "What sort of danger and where does it come from?"

Laver had run out of cards; he sat silent in an awkward misery.

"I asked you a question, Sir Richard."

"I heard you."

"And again you decline to give an answer?" The contempt was no longer hidden but overt.

Laver, in a corner, collapsed. "I was hoping you would make your own guess."

"I wouldn't have attended you if I'd known it was for a guessing game."

Richard Laver made a last snatch at dignity. "But I will give you some advice."

"That is kind." The words were not encouraging but they hadn't been a formal refusal.

"You would be wise to go abroad for a while."

... I might barely get away with that if Alistair Leech can be made to see reason.

"The same advice I gave to Van Loon." Charles Russell paused. "But of course you now know what I said to Van Loon."

Laver had retreated uneasily into the fortress of the weak man, stubbornness. "I still think you'd be wise to go."

"And hide myself?"

"I suppose so. In effect ... Well, yes."

"Any further suggestions?"

"I'm sorry I haven't."

77

"Then I wish you good morning." Charles Russell rose. He took his immaculate hat and left.

He went back to his flat and smoked a cigar. Later he took an afternoon nap. Unconscious cerebration was something he believed in firmly and when he awoke he saw it clearly. If Laver had been trying to frighten him he had succeeded in making him highly curious. But Laver himself was frightened white. Sir Richard Laver was running scared and men who were that scared did foolish things.

When Russell had gone Richard Laver sat on; he was shaking but not entirely in fear; part of it was an animal fury. He was muttering and occasionally grunting, a patient for some learner psychiatrist. The most grievous of all mental wounds had cut him very deep indeed. The name of the wound was humiliation.

By reflex he lit another link in the deathdance which he couldn't break. He ought to have been in the driving seat and instead he'd been lying flat in the road. Where had he mishandled the interview? He had made one big mistake but it hadn't been that. Even without it that man had out-gunned him. In the end he hadn't concealed his contempt. It had been headmaster, old style, and recalcitrant schoolboy.

From his misery emerged one decision: self-deception was no longer possible. He didn't envy Charles Russell, he hated his bowels.

He rang up a number in a suburb of Birmingham. "Kiernan? I'd like a word with you."

"Business, I take it."

"Certainly business."

"It's going to cost you a lot of money. If I didn't employ expensive lawyers I wouldn't still have a licence to drive. I give myself one more and that's the end. I've been saving it for the really big one. Big in price, I mean. You read me?"

"The price," Laver said, "will of course be negotiable."

"Oh no, it won't." Kiernan named a figure. "If you won't find it somebody else will."

"Very well," Richard Laver said at last. After all it would be the taxpayers' money and he was still at heart a civil servant.

"When do I see you?"

"Come tomorrow."

"I'll come tomorrow. Expect me at noon."

Catharsis, Richard Laver reflected. A salubrious discharge of emotion.

The epidemic of influenza was waning but Willy had succumbed at the tail of it. He had gone to his parents' house and collapsed where his mother had fussed but nursed him efficiently. His father had rung the Security Executive and received regrets and some formal sympathy from a man whose name he didn't know. Charles Russell, he thought a trifle sourly, would have telephoned back at once concernedly . . . Was there anything he could do?

There was not but of course that wasn't the point.

Willy was still distinctly shaky but he was conscientious and more than a little bored, and against his mother's protestations he got up and took a taxi to work. There was a note on his desk to contact Laver and he went upstairs at once to do so.

"Glad to have you back and recovered."

Willy knew that he was still looking terrible but he let the cliché pass in silence. Laver looked at his watch: it was five to twelve. "I've another appointment at twelve. I'm sorry. Was there anything much on your desk?"

"Very little."

And he'd have known that too, Willy thought as he left. Internally the Executive was efficiently run even if the head of it was not very clever at handling people.

As Willy Smith went downstairs a man who was coming up fast bumped into him. Willy stepped back to let him pass. He had met this man once at a very small conference – small because it was planning a crime. But Kiernan didn't recognise Willy; Kiernan pressed on to Sir Richard Laver.

Willy didn't go back to his desk but went home to his flat. The woman who did his cleaning was there but after ten days absence there was little to do. He sent her out to stock up the frig.

He hadn't liked what he'd seen in any way. Kiernan was a high-class killer, not a general purpose killer – a specialist. His speciality was car accidents which were not. It was an outrage that he still had a licence but he had never been drunk and had used clever lawyers. Just the same, Willy knew, he had one to go. Just one and then he was finished, done for. Whatever they did to him and that might be plenty Kiernan would not be driving for some time.

Which meant that his price would now be high, something to cushion the years when he'd lost his trade. And the Executive didn't splash it about, or hadn't in Charles Russell's time. It offered the going rate and it kept its word. But Kiernan wouldn't want that, he'd want a packet, and he wouldn't have troubled to come to London unless he'd been pretty sure of his money. So Laver was going to employ the best and probably pay through the nose to get him.

That looked disturbingly like some first-class target, somebody worth the money . . .

Charles Russell?

8

Willy's cleaning woman returned with some food and Willy Smith made himself an omelette. When he had eaten he lit a reefer, but for once it didn't clear his mind. He ground it out half smoked for he wasn't hooked. He then took paper and wrote it down as Russell had always insisted he do.

1 *Russell uses a wartime contact to get some money out of Italy.*

2 *Van Loons run a highly suspect business, or suspect to all who don't dodge their taxes.*

3 *When Karel van Loon comes over to London the Executive has him shadowed to Russell. The reason for that is known to Laver alone.*

4 *Simultaneously, and for the moment unconnected by evidence, Van Loons are being increasingly threatened.*

5 *Laver has called up an outside killer.*

Before locking this up he re-read it distastefully for he realised it took him exactly nowhere. It lucidly stated the little he knew, but it gave no solid ground for belief that it was Russell who was the killer's target. He had been taught that hunches were often useful but also that they must be promptly justified. What especially annoyed him was paragraph 4. He didn't like 'simultaneously', and 'unconnected' he liked even less. Jane Lightwater might have something from Holland but he wasn't due to see her for several days.

He thought it over and then rang her up. "Can I come and see you urgently?"

Characteristically, she didn't dither. "Wait a moment, will

you?" He waited. "Come tomorrow at nine. I'll give you break-fast."

He arrived next morning as another man left. He looked prosperous, very sure of himself, and his "Good morning" didn't sound quite English. Jane let Willy in; she was fully dressed. She wasn't the type to slop round in a dressing gown. On the table were the remains of a breakfast, slices of cold ham and cheese, three sorts of bread and a large pot of coffee. She began to clear it away unfussily. "That, as you see, was a very Dutch breakfast. I don't do that for all of them but Piet is a rather special case. I'm getting rather fond of Piet and that's a foolish thing to do." She took the tray to the kitchen but came back quickly. "Now what would you like yourself? Egg and bacon?"

"I'd rather have two boiled eggs, done soft."

"Just as you like but I won't be eating myself. I'm stuffed to the eyeballs with cheese and ham."

She brought him his eggs and a fresh pot of coffee. The eggs were perfectly done, the coffee real. "Now tell me what this is all about."

"Was that Piet I saw leaving?"

"It certainly was."

"The banker friend you mentioned before?"

"And a very worried banker too." She didn't wait to be asked but told him at once. "Piet confirms there's something explosive in Holland, the fear of another colossal scandal. Piet is a perfectly orthodox banker but there are others who are distinctly less so. And one is rumoured to be under pressure. The fear is that he'll cut and run, the rich evadees' money with him. If that happens there'll be quite a bang. An international bang at that since a lot of this money is other than Dutch."

"Did he give a name?"

"As it happens he did. It was Van Loons, the one which you mentioned yourself."

He looked at her in admiration. "You've done marvellously well, you know."

She waved it aside. "Oh, it wasn't difficult. Men talk in bed –

82

you know that already – and worried men talk even more. I didn't have to probe or pry. It all came out and it did him good."

"As no doubt did the breakfast."

She laughed. "I read you."

"You're a cousin of Charles Russell, aren't you?"

"Distantly. Who told you that?"

"Charles Russell did."

"Charles Russell would. I'm a whore but his cousin."

For the second time Willy Smith was enchanted. That was the way it worked. It really did. The old boy network included old girls and he was authentically an old boy himself.

"Do you still see him?"

"At family funerals."

"Would he come here if you asked him?"

"Surely."

"I'd like you to give him a message."

"What message?"

"I'd like you to say I've a hunch he's in danger."

"What sort of danger?"

"I said a hunch. He plays his own but dislikes other people's."

She thought it over, suddenly curious. "You have nothing to go on?"

"Only suspicion."

"Your own?"

"No, other people's. Their suspicion of Russell. And suspicion breeds just as desperate action as the facts on some office file. Often more so."

She was very quick. "Was that a slip?"

"No, it was a hint. You have taken it."

"As background information I have. But I can't put a simple suspicion as fact."

"To Russell, you mean? He would laugh if you did."

"I'll get some more coffee." She went and made it. When she returned her mood had changed; she was suddenly cool and entirely practical. "Why don't you go to Russell yourself?"

"Because you're a woman. Because you're related."

"That's not enough."

"Very well. I *have* seen him. I told him the little I knew at the time and that I'd sleep a whole lot sounder at night if he didn't make further contacts with Karel van Loon."

"And what did he say to that?"

"He thanked me. He was pleased to praise what he called my loyalty."

"Rightly," Jane Lightwater said. "Quite rightly." It was a virtue which like Russell she rated high. "And what am I to say to him now?"

"I'd like him to keep a very low profile."

She showed a flash of irritation. "I detest that sort of jargon — loathe it. My defence is to say that I don't understand it."

"Then allow me to translate into English. I'd like him to go abroad for a bit."

"You mean go into hiding?"

"More or less."

"And you think he'd listen?"

"From you he might."

"It's a pretty thin case. Just a hunch of your own."

"I realise that."

She thought it over again and then said bluntly: "You're holding something back."

"Yes, I am." He had considered telling but turned it down. He could tell her that a killer called Kiernan had been summoned to the Security Executive, but he wasn't yet sure who was Kiernan's target. He might be compromising some operation which had nothing whatever to do with Russell. He didn't believe it but there the fact was. Discipline in the end had held.

She accepted it with surprising grace. "It's for you to deal my hand. It's a poor one."

"Don't I know it."

"That's something. But since I'm rather fond of Charles Russell I'll do as you ask and I'll do it now. You can listen on the other telephone."

He picked it up and heard her dial, then Charles Russell's voice.

"Charles Russell here."

"Charles, it's Jane Lightwater."

He said at once: "It's been too long."

"You're the smoothie you always were."

"What nonsense."

"Charles, I want to talk to you."

"Gladly."

"It's business I'm afraid."

"I'm getting on."

There was an earthy and appreciative chuckle. "I'm not short of clients but I do want to talk to you."

"When shall I come?"

"Can you make it tomorrow? Seven for seven-thirty. I'll give you a meal."

"I'll look forward to that. Till then. Au revoir." He'd had another engagement but set about breaking it; he had always liked and admired Jane Lightwater.

Who returned to Willy Smith with a frown. "You're a horrible little man," she said.

He knew exactly what she was really saying. "But I do have certain modest uses."

"You have uses but no rights whatever. But I was always very fond of Charles Russell. I wondered once . . . Oh, never mind."

As he went through the door she touched his arm. "I'll ring you at midnight tomorrow."

"Thanks."

Charles Russell arrived at ten minutes past seven and kissed her since they were kissing cousins. She asked him what he would drink.

"Is there whisky?"

"There is for house-guests."

He looked round the comfortable room with pleasure. He thought it a pity she didn't like rugs but there were some fine old pieces and one good picture. She caught his inspection.

"It's mostly inherited, but one or two things I bought myself. That was before old furniture went through the roof."

"You have very good taste," Charles Russell said.

"This isn't my business room, you see."

He laughed and she laughed back. They were at ease.

"I can see you're not doing too badly."

"Well enough to think of retiring soon."

"Where would you go?"

"I've got it more or less worked out. It wouldn't be London and far less a suburb, but nor would it be a village in Norfolk. But there's a little town in Northamptonshire where there's a village house I've had my eye on. Nothing grand, nowhere near a manor, but a suitable background for a well-to-do widow."

"If you stay a widow."

"What makes you say that?"

"There's a certain air of suppressed excitement . . ."

"You're uncomfortably observant, Charles. All right, I'll come clean. I've got a steady."

"Where did you meet him?"

"Here."

He was startled but she said at once: "Don't give me all the ancient wisdoms. I know that a tart who marries one of her clients – except he's a banker and would surely say 'customers' – is normally asking for very large trouble, but in this case things are running for me. He's a Dutchman and – you won't believe this – he's got wildly, insanely hooked on hunting."

"In the American sense? Going out with a gun?"

"No, horses and hounds and comic clothes."

"You said I wouldn't believe it."

"It's true. I loathe hunting myself but I'm fond of hacking, and since I don't know a soul in darkest Northamptonshire I could provide a suitable social background for an odd foreign gent who's gone dotty on foxhunting."

"You've thought it out," he said.

"I've had to. He'll be keeping his flat in Amsterdam and keeping on his business too, but it's an easy trip and he also has partners. So most of the summer he'll spend in Holland. He's also pretty rich, which helps. We shall have to do a lot to the stables."

"A Dutchman," he said. He still didn't believe it. Maharajahs

86

went hunting and rich Argentinos, but a Dutchman in a pink coat and a reinforced hat ... He didn't want to smile but finally did.

"Don't laugh at my Piet, he's not a stereotype." She began to quote but quoted smiling.

> *"In matters of commerce*
> *The fault of the Dutch*
> *Is in giving too little*
> *And asking too much*

"But he isn't like that at all; he's generous." She touched the pearls round her neck. "These are real."

"He sounds a very nice man."

"He is. And now if you're ready perhaps we could eat."

There was an avocado with a smooth shrimp sauce and a well-chilled bottle of Mâcon Blanc. Afterwards there was *arroz cubana*, and since bananas killed any worthwhile wine a good lager in two noble bottles. They were neither of the type to chatter when good food was on the table for eating, but when they had finished Charles Russell asked her:

"Do you mind if I smoke a cigar?"

"Provided it isn't East Indian go ahead. Piet smokes those Javanese cheroots. I'm not the sort to start breaking my man in but that's something I think I'll have to bend."

"No doubt you can be extremely persuasive."

"I hope so. I've been a pretty good whore."

They laughed again, more at ease than ever. "Let's go and sit down. I'll clear up later."

She gave him a glass of Armagnac and Russell came to the point as he drank it. "I take it you didn't ask me for my *beaux yeux*."

"You're still a remarkably handsome man, but no, there was another reason."

"Shoot it," he said.

"William Wilberforce Smith – of course you'll remember him."

"Of course I do. It was I who appointed him."

"He thinks the sun shines out of your bottom."

"I'm afraid he does. It's sometimes embarrassing."

"He's also my regular weekly contact but yesterday he called unofficially. Since he's tactful he didn't bring any money. I took the point at once."

"I'm sure."

"Willy Smith is a worried man. About you."

"Did he say why?"

"He's lumbered with an enormous hunch."

"He's a little young to be playing hunches."

"He's the same age as I am – thirty-one." In fact she was thirty-six but looked less. She had always taken very good care of herself.

"So what's his hunch?"

"That someone is after you."

"He told me that himself."

"And what did you say?"

"I thanked him for his consideration."

"Which amounted to a snub."

"Unintended."

"Anyway, he comes to me, unofficially as I've told you already, and begs me to rub in the message of danger."

"Did he give a specific reason?"

"No. But he was holding something back. He admitted it."

"I'm glad to hear he's not quite mad. He's been sailing too close to the wind already. The Executive is about *security*."

"Also it's not what it used to be."

"I've heard rumours," Charles Russell admitted reluctantly. They were too widespread to be blandly denied.

"Laver is a twerp."

"Not quite. He's a frightened man as are many officials. They're frightened for their image, their jobs. They're frightened for their promotion – the rat race."

"And frightened men – "

"You needn't go on."

She watched him as he drank the Armagnac, thinking as Phyllis Leech had thought that he wasn't a man to be scared of shadows.

He was healthy for his age and still virile; he wouldn't engage a
danger unnecessarily but he would probably prefer a bullet to a
stroke and being a permanent burden. He said at length:

"You're holding back too."

If he had expected to embarrass her the words threw the opposite switch with a bang. She was suddenly on the Inquisitor's
throne, asking Russell the questions, demanding plain answers.

"You've had contacts with a bank called Van Loons?"

"I have, and they were more or less innocent. I told Willy that
when he came to see me."

"But there are people who might not think them innocent?"

"I suppose that's true. At least in theory."

"You know Karel van Loon is being threatened?"

"Again it was I who told Willy that."

"Then I'll tell you something else more interesting and it
doesn't come from Willy Smith. It comes from my Piet who has
no reason to lie to me. Karel van Loon is thinking of running –
running with the loot, the lot. What's legally his and the stuff
he's concealing."

"Is he indeed?" Russell thought it over. "One piece of news
deserves another – several in fact, so listen carefully." He ground
out his cigar; he had had enough. "Since Willy saw me I've seen
Van Loon a second time. He came to me of his own volition and
asked me to help him against his enemies. Naturally I turned it
down. But that interview was bugged by the Security Executive,
who later called me up and tried to get tough."

"That's an awful lot in a single sentence."

He repeated it, spacing the facts out carefully.

"Does Willy know this?"

"I should hardly think so."

"May I tell him, then?" She had promised to do so anyway but
was relieved when Russell said:

"Yes, by all means. In fact I'd be rather glad if you did."

"Suppose he comes charging round again, insisting that you
go abroad?"

He said placidly: "I might even consider it. From what you
tell me something is brewing up nastily and nature didn't make

me a hero. But before I go and hide myself I'd want something stronger, some concrete evidence."

"That evidence could come too late."

"I see what you mean. Yes, that's perfectly true."

He took his leave and she waited till midnight, ringing Willy Smith as she'd promised. He listened in a total silence and Jane Lightwater had to prompt him.

"What now?"

"He said he might consider going away?"

"But not without evidence, concrete evidence."

Telling him that an accident-fixer had been calling at the Executive could easily – fatally – fall short of this. Russell might very well admit that the call could have a sinister edge to it but he would also point out that it could be simply coincidence, some operation unconnected with the Executive's late head. When he said 'concrete' he mostly meant 'watertight'. Willy said what Jane had herself:

"The proof he wants could come too late."

"I told him that myself. He took the point."

"But didn't pursue it."

"He's as proud as the devil." A pause, then in a different voice: "Willy, can't you think of something? I'm fond of him and I know you are too."

"An understatement," he said.

"There's no time to be clever. Go to bed and think it over."

"Excellent advice. I will. And in passing you're a very nice woman."

But he didn't go to bed at once; he took from the locked drawer of his desk the Appreciation he'd made the day before, adding two paragraphs, writing smoothly and confidently.

6 *Since I spoke to him Russell has talked to Van Loon again. The Executive took that sufficiently seriously to have the interview bugged in Russell's flat.*

7 *It then sent for Russell and tried to scare him.*

8 *Karel van Loon is thinking of running.*

He considered this: in its way it was admirable. But the paragraphs were now misnumbered. *Laver has called up an outside killer* should now be number 9, not 5.

Admirable it might be but useless since it lacked the essential glue, a motive. It was a record of highly suspicious events, it suggested that someone suspected Russell. The Executive of its own motion? Improbable. Assuming there'd been a breach of the law it was one against the Inland Revenue and the Executive wasn't the Revenue's creature. Only two men could give it firm orders...

It came to him like a flash in the sky. Some big boy had his money in Holland, much bigger than that odious bishop. He suspected Charles Russell of interfering, perhaps of blowing the story and breaking him. He was protecting himself – that was it, *protection* – and he was leaning on Richard Laver to do it.

He must be a Very Big Boy indeed.

William Wilberforce Smith burnt his précis carefully. One should never keep unnecessary paper, especially in a drawer at home. He seldom drank but now poured a neat whisky. He needed to sleep and mistrusted all sedatives.

Tomorrow would be a busy day.

The first visit he made was one to Fleet Street, where he called on a lady who ran a 'Court and Society' on a newspaper which cared for neither. It was a well-paid job but also frustrating and she welcomed Willy Smith with some warmth. They had met before and had got on well. In her own peculiar jargon she thought him a dish.

"I want to check a man's movements."

"I'm not a detective."

"His social movements, I mean – where he might go."

"Then you'll have to give me his background."

"I will. His name is Colonel Charles Russell – "

"I've heard of him. He has a piece in the morgue but he isn't yet dead." She had done this before and knew the drill. "Habits and interests, please."

"Habits regular and interests varied."

"Such as?"

"Fishing and golf."

She shook her well-groomed head at once. "Fishing is out — there's been a drought. Nobody's putting a fly on the rivers."

"Then golf perhaps?"

She looked at a list. "There's a meeting of the Seniors at Woking today."

It sounded hot but on reflection wasn't. If Kiernan's strike was going to be Woking, Willy would have no time to meet it, but he didn't really think it would be. Russell would be home in daylight and Kiernan had always struck at night.

"Anything even faintly military?"

The girl looked at another list. "There is. There's a do at the Staff College tomorrow evening. Was he there?"

"I imagine so. He made full Colonel."

"Any idea of the date?"

"We could work it out roughly. Assuming he was a bright young Captain — "

She looked at her list again. "That doesn't matter. This do is for over-sixties only."

"Then it's going to be an enormous party. There are generals all over the country in shoals."

"I doubt if very many will go. The really senior ones will be pretty decrepit and the rest of them hate each other's guts. I'd put it at twenty or twenty-five."

"What are the arrangements?"

"Simple. A couple of drinks at the Staff College first, then off to the Hilltops hotel for dinner."

"Who will probably have a list of guests."

"I imagine so." She looked at him shrewdly. "You're planning to use me. What's it worth?"

"A damned good lunch at wherever you fancy."

"Very well, I'll check."

She proceeded to do so. She rang the Hilltops hotel and gave the name of her paper, asking to speak to the manager personally. It took a minute or two to find and connect him, but once on she hooked and gaffed him efficiently . . . Her paper was interested in a dinner at the Hilltops, a dinner next evening for eminent officers. They might even be sending a man down to cover it, a photographer too if sufficiently interesting, but of course she would have to ask her editor and in any case the great man's decision would no doubt depend on the names of the guests.

The manager was loudly delighted. The Hilltops was not at the top of the list of the countrywide chain which had recently bought it and this publicity would do him much good. He read out the names and she wrote them down. Colonel Charles Russell was seventeenth.

Willy bought her the generous luncheon he'd promised and then took her back to her office by taxi. She was agreeably tipsy and mildly amorous. He had what he believed he wanted but he liked to double check and did it. Charles Russell would not be getting drunk but he would certainly have taken wine and a car was part of his way of life. The last thing he'd wish would be losing his licence so he would surely hire a car for the evening.

From the Yellow Pages he made a list of car-hire firms close to Russell's flat, then took a taxi to Marylebone confidently. He could assume the manner of a plain-clothes policeman and had never been asked to show his warrant. This was as well since he didn't have one. At the first two firms he drew a blank but at the third he got his confirmation. Yes, a Colonel Russell had booked a car. Tomorrow evening at six o'clock. To go to the Staff College, Camberley, first, then on to the Hilltops hotel for dinner. A Cortina and an experienced driver.

Willy went home and collected his Alfa for he had still to make the necessary reconnaissance. It was now latish in the afternoon but that suited Willy Smith very well. It would be dark by the time he got to Camberley and if the action were going to take place in darkness the reconnaissance should be made in it too.

If the action ... He gave it a careless shrug. He might be wasting his time but Willy thought not. The alarm bells were ringing loud and insistently.

He didn't bother with the College itself since the route from it to the Hilltops hotel ran through the town in short broken stretches which prohibited sufficient speed for an accident to be certain of killing. He went directly to the Hilltops hotel.

It had once been a large Edwardian villa, the type favoured by generals who were also rich men, then a modest residential hotel for the widows of those generals' sons. Later it had grown by accretion and now advertised as a venue for Conferences. A second bar had been added, all brass and chrome, with a barmaid who was hardly less brassy, beyond it two committee rooms furnished with mid-Atlantic severity. The chairman's chair was bigger than all the rest. A neon arrow pointed to BANQUETING ROOM and the menu was on a table in the hall.

Willy Smith went in and bought a drink. Three Africans were there already, drinking with a faint air of bravado. One of them half rose but sat down again. Willy put them as Nigerians, probably cadets from Sandhurst. In which case they were running a considerable risk, though less of a risk than if they'd been white. Their colour would protect them effectively. Given a coloured skin and Commonwealth status they were unlikely to be dismissed from Sandhurst short of spitting in the Commandant's eye.

Willy, third generation British, resented that as discrimination.

He had bought a drink to avoid too much notice but his real interest was not the hotel's interior. He took his drink outside and walked around. There was limited parking in front of the portico, but on a night with any sort of party they would have to use the main car park behind. Willy followed the sign and nodded approvingly. There was parking for thirty or forty cars in an area which would suit him perfectly. It was surrounded by typical Surrey scrub, rhododendrons which had long been neglected, behind them stunted birch and heather. He noted it wasn't overlooked except by some windows at the back of the hotel, and for the moment the room behind them was dark. The park was almost empty now but tomorrow it would be almost full.

He threw away what was left of his drink, taking the tumbler back to the bar. He drove to the railway station, noting the distance. Say a couple of miles – half an hour on foot. The 21.35 from Waterloo would bring him to the hotel by eleven o'clock. They wouldn't be likely to finish before, and Charles Russell seldom sat late over wine.

9

The train Willy had chosen was not in the rush hours and put him down at Camberley on time. He walked briskly to the Hilltops hotel, taking five minutes less than the thirty he had allowed himself. He went half way up the Hilltops drive, then faded into the shrubs which bordered it. He slipped through these to the back and the car park.

He noticed a stroke of good fortune at once for this evening the room at the back was lighted and from it came occasional laughter, the hum of a discreet sort of revelry. The night was warm with a threat of rain and there was a gap for air in the big room's curtains. Willy worked his way along the wall.

Inside they had clearly drunk the loyal toast for most of the men were smoking cigars. They were in dinner jackets and quite informal but at the head of the table a man was speaking. Willy could see Russell clearly. He had the frozen look of complete, polite boredom.

Willy decided to give him ten minutes.

He had spotted the Cortina at once, the only one there. It was parked at the edge, the rhododendrons behind it, which made his task that much the easier. But the driver was not the man he'd expected but a young woman reading a book by the inside light. Willy didn't much fancy assaults on women but in his pocket were the tools of his trade. Whatever he must do he'd do mercifully.

The young woman was reading a Spanish phrasebook for she wished to surprise her Spanish lover. He had told her he was an unmarried man though in fact he had a wife and three children.

95

The lie had not disturbed his conscience. Like most Spaniards he despised all foreigners, and deep in his unexplored subconscious was the knowledge that the English were heretics, deeper still that they had destroyed his empire. If their women shared their beds incontinently that was hardly more than a local convenience in a country he sincerely detested. The act barely counted, wasn't worth a confession.

Willy looked at his watch and made his move. He opened the door of the car and slipped in. He was wearing a hood and gloves.

The young woman was frightened but kept her head. "If it's money you're after I've very little. And if it's rape I know some judo."

"It isn't rape and it isn't money."

"Then what do you want?"

"I want your car."

"It isn't mine."

"It doesn't matter." He was talking to relax her guard but feeling in his left-hand pocket. He found what he wanted and pulled it out. For a second or two she struggled wildly, then went limp as a doll across the steering wheel.

Willy got out and opened the driver's door. She was light and he carried her weight quite easily, laying her out with some care, almost ritually. He didn't bother to tie her up. He knew that she'd wake in half an hour and half an hour was more than enough. In half an hour they'd be on the main road to London; in half an hour they might also be dead. It depended how good a driver Kiernan was.

He went back to the Cortina and opened the bonnet. He knew that these hire cars often had governors and he had simple tools in his right hand pocket. There was a stopper which held her down to fifty-five.

Willy removed it, then climbed back in the car. There were other drivers in other cars but all of them seemed still asleep. The noise of the party was sharply decreasing.

Charles Russell opened the car door and slid in. He was far from drunk but had taken wine, and for a second he didn't notice the

96

hooded man. When he did he said much the same as the woman had.

"I've a few pounds and a watch and a silver lighter. Hardly worth a stiff sentence if they happen to catch you."

"Explanations as we go along, sir. For the moment belt up and I'll do the talking."

The voice which had answered was unmistakably Willy's and it couldn't have been considered unusual if Russell had shown some mild surprise. Instead he continued the conversation.

"Like another and much more eminent person I'll never belt up till the law obliges me. I'd much sooner go through the screen than fry. I saw it in the war once. Horrible. Fighter on fire on the ground and the pilot jammed in it."

"I've heard that the RAF sometimes shot them."

"This one they didn't and he wasn't my officer."

William Wilberforce Smith was admiring Russell and Charles Russell was admiring Willy. Willy was thinking that here was Russell, his driver inexplicably vanished and a man in a hood and gloves at her wheel. And he was chatting as though he had been in his club. Russell was thinking that here was Willy, dressed up like some clown in a comic strip but as innocent of melodrama as a fine actor underplaying Hamlet.

They had moved from the car park and joined a queue past the portico. Other cars were picking up, and they were stopping and re-starting again till the head of the queue was finally clear. Willy had tensed and Russell felt it. He might be wrong about Kiernan's plan after all, and in that case they were a sitting target. But once on the road he relaxed and spoke.

"Have you heard of a man called Kiernan?"

"Yes. I remember I employed him once. He's a specialist in accidents which are not."

"We're his Target for Tonight."

"Indeed? Do you know on whose orders?"

"I'll give you one guess."

A silence for several seconds, then: "Reluctantly I have made one guess. Why didn't you just warn me, though?"

"You demanded proof and you're not easy to wheedle."

97

"I apologise for being tiresome. So here the proof comes?"

"I'm afraid it does. And I thought you should have a competent driver."

"I'm increasingly in your debt, Willy Smith. And the lady who was driving this car?"

"Will come to in about another ten minutes. I assure that she's quite unharmed."

"That's my boy."

They were cruising along the London road and Willy was watching his mirror intently. Their speed was much below the average and one or two cars honked and passed them irritably. Presently Russell asked:

"What's his plan?"

"He'll come fast from behind and try to ditch us. Turn us over if he can manage that too."

"And you're sure you can prevent it?"

"Reasonably sure. I was a rally driver once and he wasn't."

"Professionally? I didn't know that."

"It wasn't worth mentioning. It was while I was wasting my time in the City. My mother hated it but my father was for it. It gave him a whole lot to boast about and he let me have the money I wanted till I was good enough to pick up some sponsoring. By then I learnt a few tricks which the amateur doesn't know."

"This isn't much of a car for tricks on the road."

"It's the one you brought and that's the end of it. Use another and it could be traced to me."

"And what are you going to do with this one?"

"Dump it discreetly somewhere in London."

"And me?"

"I'm afraid you'll have to thumb a lift."

"In a dinner jacket?"

"Why not in a dinner jacket? You made a pass at a lady who pushed you out. You'll be giving some stranger a happy giggle."

Charles Russell nodded: the plan stood up . . . Hooded villain knocks out driver of car, then snatches her fare and drives him off, presumably to rob him later. Somewhere on the road some-

98

thing happens. Villain loses his nerve and ejects his passenger. The car is later found abandoned.

... Somewhere on the road something happens.

"You spoke of my thumbing a lift. I don't object. Provided, that is, I'm alive to do so."

"There may be a little bumping and boring but I'm prepared to bet we both survive it."

"You sound confident."

"Or I wouldn't be here."

They were still cruising quietly, Willy watching the mirror. Presently:

"That's him behind us."

"How do you know?"

"From the way he's driving. It's a biggish car, a Mercedes, I think, and Mercs don't hang about behind Cortinas."

"Why's he hanging at all?"

"He doesn't mean to ram from behind. That would give him at best an even chance. No, he's waiting for the stretch he's picked for it. In a couple of miles there's a built-up causeway. He'll do his best to push us off it. If we went through the guardrail we'd be sure to turn over. In which case he'd come down too and set us on fire."

"In which case I'd be glad of no belt."

"Please yourself but I'm happier belted myself. I went rallying belted – you weren't allowed not to – and it gives me a sort of conditioned assurance."

He had raised the speed to sixty-five, pacing the Cortina like a horse in a steeplechase.

He knows his business, Charles Russell thought.

"Two hundred yards," Willy said, then: "He's coming."

Behind them the big Merc had pulled out. It drew level with an arrogant ease, dangerously close, almost touching.

William Wilberforce Smith put his right hand down expertly. There was a sickening scream of tearing metal. The driver of the Mercedes flinched. He braked and dropped behind again.

Charles Russell lit his last cigar. "I've never driven a car to kill but I imagine that was pretty close."

"It's a matter of whose nerve goes first, and also of not over-doing the medicine. If I'd hit him much harder we shouldn't be moving still."

The Mercedes was still behind them sulkily.

"What happens now?"

"There's a bridge might suit him."

It had begun to rain and Willy switched on the wipers. Russell asked him:

"A disadvantage?"

"On the contrary it gives me an extra trick." Willy was calm and coolly professional. "We're going to need that extra trick. Next time he comes he knows I won't flinch, but neither can I nudge him much harder. He could tear the side off this one easily. I wouldn't mind that if you wouldn't either, but I would mind if we jammed a wheel. He'd have us then where he wants us. Cold."

"What are you going to do?"

"I'll show you. That's where the rain comes in and helps. That bridge is a mile. I wish you'd belt up."

They were still doing sixty-five fairly comfortably with a top speed, in a pinch, of maybe eighty. But Willy wasn't concerned with speed – the Merc could eat him at that game and Willy knew it; he was concerned with a moment's acceleration. The next time the Merc pulled out he trod on it and for a second they were two lengths ahead. Simultaneously he spun the wheel. The Cortina skidded across the Mercedes's bonnet. The Mercedes braked fiercely and Willy corrected. He did it as he changed down, in one movement.

"Looks easy," Russell said.

"It is when you've done it a hundred times. You practise it on a greasepan, you know, and this road at the moment is just about that."

The bridge was past them but the Mercedes behind still. "He's persistent," Russell said.

"He's being paid plenty. But we're getting pretty close to London and as the traffic thickens it gets more difficult. He can't risk a crash with an oncoming car."

"There's one fast stretch ahead."

"I know there is."

Willy Smith knew but was inclined to discount it. This stretch was flat and fast and modern, but its level wasn't anywhere higher than the level of the ground around it. Kiernan might very well force them off it but he couldn't guarantee to topple them. He knew now that Russell's driver drove well and a half-job wouldn't suit his purpose.

Willy considered what cards Kiernan held. He had advantages in both pace and weight but the deadly ball and chain of lack of choice. He must strike here or not again tonight, for beyond this last clear stretch was suburbia, traffic lights and crossing lorries, the car which shot out of its owner's garage. What would he do if he were Kiernan? Frankly, he'd call it a night and go home. But he wasn't Kiernan, he wasn't yet desperate. As Willy saw it Kiernan had one move left. He could use his speed and weight in a gamble; he would overtake, then pull half across. His car was heavily built, the Cortina wasn't. The Mercedes had English right-hand drive. Kiernan might just walk away: they would not. The front of their hire car would crumple like paper, the engine would be in their laps. He had seen it.

So stop and face it out? They were two to one ... Not on. Russell was no longer young and Willy knew that he never carried a weapon. Kiernan killed by rigging accidents but Kiernan was close to losing his head. Willy knew it with an utter certitude as he'd known in the last miles of a rally that the man behind him was going to do something foolish on a bend.

Bend. Curve. Bend. A bell rang faintly. This one was fast and ordinarily safe but not so gentle you could see right through it. And the rain was now a blinding downpour, the wipers beating the windscreen dementedly.

The faint bell was now a clamorous warning. Roadworks ahead and single-line traffic. He had noticed them on his recce last night. He had been driving in the other lanes but in these two there'd be a queue of traffic. He had driven this road and if Kiernan had not ... The roadworks would be lighted but in this rain ...

He pushed the accelerator down to the floorboards. The Mercedes behind at once responded. It did more, it began to overtake. It was a bonnet ahead, then half a length.

He's committed, Willy thought – he's had it. He's had it if he can't slip behind again. I do not intend that he slip behind again. ... I hope this car has decent brakes.

They were better than he had expected, much better, and Russell hit his head on the windscreen. He hit it hard but didn't break it. In front there was an echoing crash. Russell had got back to his seat.

Willy pulled out to pass the wreck. It was lying on its righthand side, the driver pinned below the wheel. It wasn't on fire and Willy was glad of it. He didn't like Kiernan in any way but he was glad that he wouldn't burn to death.

He put some miles between himself and the wreck before he pulled in to examine Russell.

"Are you all right, sir?"

"I'll tell you later."

Willy could see no sign of real damage but the speech was shaky and blurred with shock. I can't possibly leave him now, Willy thought. I'll have to take him home.

Change of plan.

How serious? He considered carefully. One aspect hadn't changed at all. That girl would recover consciousness quickly and if she didn't know the name of her fare her company would have it recorded. The police would question Russell as a matter of course. And what would Russell say? That hadn't changed either. Willy had kept his hood on deliberately since it made it that much easier for Russell.

... "Did you recognise the man who snatched you, sir?"

"He wore a hood and gloves throughout."

"His voice perhaps?"

Willy laughed aloud. Russell was much too fly for that. He seldom lied – he did it poorly and knew it – but he was excellent at convincing half-answers. He would say that the voice *had* seemed familiar, but it had spoken with an educated accent and there were perhaps five million people who still did that. The police must not expect Charles Russell, who'd been head of the Security Executive, to take a blind chance on five million people. The police might suspect but they wouldn't dare press him.

What had been lost was a touch of the plausible, the pushing Russell out to thumb a lift. But the damage to the Cortina compensated. Russell had bumped his head on the windscreen (he wouldn't mind saying that, it was true) and you had to be very hard indeed to leave an elderly man in the rain with concussion, to say nothing of what might hit you later if the elderly man should happen to die. So the mugger had robbed him but had driven him home.

Abandoning a damaged car later? The police could connect with the Merc in theory for there'd be the Cortina's paint on the wrecked Mercedes and the Mercedes's paint on the abandoned Cortina. In a tale of detection it would happen inevitably but it was very unlikely to happen this evening. Stolen cars littered northern London nightly and the Mercedes's crash had been miles to the west of it. Going too fast in the rain. You bought it. There would be nothing for even a jack in a story to put the forensic machine into gear.

Willy went over Charles Russell carefully. He took his money, his watch and his silver lighter. Charles Russell didn't ask questions but smiled. He seemed to be recovering from the worst of the immediate shock and Willy said:

"I'll be driving you home. But we don't want anyone else to see me. Can you get yourself upstairs to bed – without me, I mean, or waking your housekeeper?"

"I can try," Russell said. His speech was clearing.

Willy drove to Russell's flat and got out. There wasn't a soul in the street nor a lighted window. Russell needed an arm up the short flight of steps.

"Give me your keys."

Willy opened the door.

"Good luck, sir."

"Many, many thanks."

When Russell had shut the door behind him Willy went back to the car and drove away. He stopped round the corner and took off the hood; he folded it, with the gloves, in his pockets. Then he drove into north London's jungle and abandoned the car in a silent side street.

He began his long walk home till the tubes should open. He wasn't going to risk a taxi. A prowling policeman eyed him suspiciously but Willy's clothes and his "Good morning, officer" reassured him that this wasn't a housebreaker. He had been on this beat for several years and had already made one bad mistake.

It's my lucky night, Willy thought – it really is. I really believe I've got away with it.

And so he very probably would have but for two things which he hadn't considered. One was a slip he had made himself, a slip in the car with the girl who'd been driving it. The other he had no reason to think of. It was the malice of a single woman, the malice of Mrs Phyllis Leech.

10

Mrs Phyllis Leech read two morning newspapers. The first was mostly considered serious, and Phyllis Leech often found it pompous; the second was the tabloid *Clarion*, a lot less aloof but a lot more readable. This morning she read the heavy first and, surprisingly, the first leading article. It was a masterpiece of its curious kind, balanced and making few direct statements, obviously carefully read for libel. But if you could read between the costive lines the message was rather clearer than most.

Mr Alistair Leech was on the skids and accelerating every day. She frowned but not in dissent; she knew it. She had her own listening lines into active politics and knew he was very near the edge. The Ginger Job was remorselessly hunting him and the bobbery pack which whined at his heels. That was bad but it was nothing new: at that sort of skirmish Leech was experienced. What was dangerous was loss of grip in Cabinet. The last meeting had been touch and go and more than one senior man was hedging his bets.

She wondered what would happen when he went. He might conceivably ask for a dissolution, which would probably sink his party for a decade, but even if he dared to ask for it, it wasn't by any means certain he'd get it. The lady whom he'd be obliged to ask would be well-briefed with all the awkward questions . . . Was there not still a fair working majority? Elections cost money and upset the neighbours. If he put on his statesman manner she'd freeze him and if he tried to bully she'd have him thrown out.

Mrs Alistair Leech much admired this lady. Their styles of life were notably different but both of them knew their own minds and followed them.

No, Alistair wouldn't play for the big one which in any case he wouldn't win. The polls showed his party lagging badly, and though polls were often sensationally wrong the other portents pointed similarly. His party would be cut down to a rump and he himself could lose his seat.

There was also the man himself to consider. He wasn't one to go with a bang, some resounding appeal to the party's grassroots which she was privately sure he would lose ignominiously; he was more likely to go with a sad, sad whimper, some excuse about a breakdown in health. There would be medical comings and goings to build it up, hints in the less unfriendly newspapers. Finally the reluctant announcement: the Prime Minister's health had broken down in selfless service to his country and party. His doctors had insisted he must retire.

Which wouldn't suit Phyllis Leech at all. Just the same she could make a life. They were rich.

She turned to the *Clarion* with a sense of relief. The front page was about some scandal in football with a picture of a manager sacked, other pictures of players who'd at last been suspended. But inside were the titbits she loved, and one of them caught her eye immediately.

EX SECURITY CHIEF ESCAPES IN ROAD ACCIDENT.

One of the reasons for Charles Russell's success had been his unvaryingly good relations with the Press. He had seldom been able to give the whole story, but neither had he hidden pompously behind vague talk about the national interest. He had mostly given a story – *a* story – and from a nursing home in Ealing now, under the watchful eye of Dame Molly Pegg, he had proceeded to give a perfect example of the use of one truth to conceal another ... Yes, it was perfectly true he'd been mugged and the experience had not been agreeable. He had told the police what he knew which was little, for the mugger had worn a hood and gloves. No, his concussion was not the result of a coshing. On the contrary, there had been an accident. A car had hit them sideways hard and Russell remembered hitting the windscreen. At the time it hadn't seemed very serious but he didn't remember

106

events very clearly till waking in his own bed next morning. It seemed there had been some delayed reaction for his housekeeper had sent for Dame Molly Pegg. So here he was in experienced hands and feeling a good deal better, thank you.

Phyllis Leech read this little piece and swore. She knew nothing of William Wilberforce Smith, she had no inside knowledge like Richard Laver, but she had told her husband to tell Richard Laver that it would suit all three, Richard Laver included, if Russell could be discreetly eliminated. A road accident, she thought – quite good. But it wasn't good at all to have bungled it. Russell was still alive and a danger.

She sent for her husband to attend her immediately. She could have rung him on the intercom but she did it in the way most humiliating. She sent her maid with an oral message. Then she went on with her breakfast deliberately.

He appeared in five minutes, fully dressed; he liked to get up early and nap after lunch.

"Have you seen the *Clarion*?"

He said a little stuffily: "I do not read the *Clarion* often." In fact it had often mauled him savagely.

"No, I know what you read and it makes me puke, but come down to earth for once and read that."

She passed him the paper and the Prime Minister read it. She watched his face as he did it intently, for by now she could read the least change of expression. They went across his face in three waves, realisation first and then alarm. Finally a sort of mulish indifference. At last he said what she had feared he would say, the comment which took them precisely nowhere.

"What of it?" he asked.

She was tempted to slap his face but restrained herself. "Are you telling me you haven't cottoned?"

"There's a possible explanation I do not like."

She found it was harder still not to hit him. "I don't like it either. I'll tell you why. I can stand for it when you lose your job. We're passing rich – I'll find other amusements. What I won't stand for is losing our money. We're agreed that Charles Russell might do just that. So what are you going to do?"

107

He shook his head.

Infirm of purpose give me the daggers.

But she was a realist and recovered promptly. She wasn't living in feudal Scotland and Alistair Leech was not Macbeth. If she pressed him he would give reasonable answers, answers which would stand up against tantrums. He would say that no second attempt was possible, or not possible for a considerable time. Charles Russell, too, could make simple deductions, and whatever he might be saying to newspapers the odds were that he'd guessed near the truth. In which case he would have early warning; he wouldn't go driving at night alone nor in lonely places even by day. It was possible he might also be guarded. It was known that there were men who worshipped him.

These arguments were much too solid to be brushed aside by tears or temper, but she was entitled to show her real alarm.

"Some of that money is mine."

"I know."

"I've also got quite a bit still in England. Then there's jewellery I've been quietly collecting while you pretended to look the other way. On top of that my present lover is rich."

"Well?" he asked wearily.

"Not well for you. If you lose that money of mine in Holland you won't get a penny from me. Not a stiver. You can live on your wretched pension and rot you. I'll be off to the sun and I won't go alone."

A man, she was thinking, would surely have beaten her, something she mightn't have found distasteful, but her husband merely said:

"Have you finished?"

"Get to hell out of here before I belt you. Go and ring Laver and give him the sack. Get yourself a competent man."

Her anger had been savage and genuine but she controlled it and began to think coolly. She had excellent connections in politics and she knew that her husband was under pressure. Pressure from the egghead Left and some of that was less than egghead, Marxist behind the progressive screen. And how would her husband cope with that? He was fond of office, which suited her well, but he hadn't the guts for an honest fight. Instead he would try to buy them off, making sham concessions and some more real. Peters would have to go from the Home Office; he had recently been tough in a race riot and that had been resented Left of him. Lord Puttock had in any case had it; he was an old-fashioned nonconformist radical as out of place in this day and age as a Webb in a top hat and a winding sheet.

She lit a cigarette and smoked most of it. Purged of anger she was almost serene, reviewing affairs with a limpid clarity. She had judged too quickly, overrunning the ball. Her husband wouldn't play his doctors till he'd played every other card in his hand, the concessions, the fixes, the open defeats. Humiliation? The man seemed to thrive on it. She would give him six months before the Ginger Job got him and six months would be enough for her purpose. That money in Holland? She shrugged resignedly. It was her instinct that she was going to lose it, if not through Russell then through some other disaster. But she still had that more than a little in England and that jewellery which she had chosen carefully. Above all she still had John who was rich. John was besotted – she'd seen to that.

In her moment of unaccustomed peace her thoughts slipped back to Sir Richard Laver. He would go like Peters and honest old Puttock, thrown from the sleigh to appease the wolves. Maybe he'd be the first to be sacrificed and in her odd way that offended her ethos. For he wasn't a bad little shit, just a nobody. It was impossible to like the man but he wasn't an object of proper hatred. He was a hierarchic man in a frozen hierarchy who had done what the boss had told him and failed. 'Them was my orders,' she thought. Some NCO. 'I swore an oath.' Some senior officer. To consider a motive was out of context.

She almost hoped they would find him another job since he could hardly go back to the civil service. There was something going in race relations . . .

Race Relations would suit Laver perfectly, his knighthood would be an asset there. He would sit on wet committees and listen to bores, he would be level-headed and fair and generally intolerable. She uttered an unmistakable raspberry. He was a rat in a trap and would be happy with others.

Alistair Leech had left with his head down. If he didn't ring Laver his wife would flay him but he didn't intend to dismiss him; he didn't dare. Instead he approached the matter obliquely, something he was very good at.

"Have you read the *Clarion* this morning?"

"It's not my newspaper."

"It is this morning – read it carefully. And when you have done so make a note. A note of my extreme displeasure."

Four telephones stood on Laver's desk though two of them were rarely used. Laver would have been much offended if it were suggested that they were symbols of status but in fact they were exactly that. He believed himself above such pretensions but at heart he was insecure and uncertain and these telephones gave him reassurance.

One of them rang and he picked it up. A voice said: "Laver?"

"Laver speaking."

Sir Richard was already furious and now he was more than a little offended. He had recognised the voice at once for it was that of a very senior policeman. Laver took conscious pride that he wasn't a snob but like many who thought of that cliché consciously at heart he was uneasily class conscious. A policeman, be he never so senior, shouldn't simply be ringing him up as 'Laver'. And Jack Pallant had been close to Russell. Their empires had often touched but never clashed. In some way inexplicable that made it worse. Pallant was saying:

"Let's use the scrambler."

Both men pressed their buttons together. There was a sort of muffled roar, then silence.

"Are you receiving me?"

"Loud and clear."

Jack Pallant had once pounded a beat and he looked back on it with a real nostalgia. It had taught him much of human nature, including such natures as Richard Laver's. "I've a rum one here from the Surrey police. They passed it to me since it concerned Charles Russell, so of course I'm passing it on in turn. Russell has been mixed up in an accident."

"I hope he's all right," Richard Laver said. His voice was concerned but not for Russell. 'Mixed-up' was not the same as being dead.

"At this moment he's in a smallish nursing home. He concussed himself in the accident but got himself back to his flat and to bed. He says he felt fairly all right at the time, but as often happens there was a reaction next morning. His housekeeper found him more or less out, and knowing what he thinks of doctors she telephoned to a friend, Molly Pegg."

"Dame Molly Pegg? I've heard of her."

"Who hasn't? Where was I? Oh yes, with Russell. So Dame Molly fixes him up with an ex-nurse friend who still has a private place in Ealing. All he needs is rest and nursing."

"What happened?" Laver asked. He must know.

"Russell tells a straightforward story. He'd been down to Camberley for some military dinner and when he came out his woman driver had gone. In her place was a man in a hood who drove him off. He robbed him of the little he had on him, then told him he meant to dump him to walk it. But he didn't because they had an accident. A car overtook them, driven insanely; it almost pushed them off the road. They banged pretty hard and Russell, who wasn't belted, shot forward. He hit his head on the windscreen and didn't break it, but he hit it hard enough for concussion. The man in the hood was then in a quandary, since if he now dumped Russell and Russell died, the charge, if he were ever caught, was going to be very much worse than R with V. So he drove him home and left the car in north London."

"Any identification?"

"None. Russell never saw his face and there weren't any prints. He wore gloves throughout."

"He must have spoken."

"He spoke all right. Russell says he spoke educated English. And that's the lot except for one thing. The man was coloured."

"How do you know?"

"He made a slip when he was doing the driver. He did it very well, by the way – just the right amount of anaesthetic to keep her quiet while he got away. Either he'd done it before or he'd been trained. Be that as it may he made a slip. The girl resisted, though not for long, and rucked up the mugger's sleeve. She noticed that the wrist was black."

"Not much of a lead."

"No, nowadays none. But that wasn't the end of a rather odd night. Do you happen to know a man called Kiernan?"

The voice had imperceptibly changed and Laver, who wasn't normally sensitive, was for once enough keyed up to notice it . . . A lie would be too dangerous since Pallant had been friendly with Russell and might know something of Kiernan's past employment. Sir Richard Laver decided to compromise.

"I've heard of him," he said.

"I thought you might have. Well, he ran into some roadworks last night on the very same road as Russell was mugged on. From the wreck he must have been going like hell and also it was raining buckets."

"Is he dead?" Laver asked. He was controlling his voice. The last thing he wanted to show was anxiety.

"I'm afraid he's very dead indeed."

"Well, thank you for letting me know."

"Not at all." A silence then unexpectedly: "Watch it."

"I beg your pardon?" Laver was trembling.

"I said to watch it. If I were you I'd watch it carefully."

Jack Pallant rang off and Laver fought himself. He sent for black coffee and drank it greedily.

. . . That policeman is holding something back.

Laver was perfectly right: Jack Pallant was. The police had had no need of forensics, no matchings of scraping of paint, no mysteries. For before he had died Paddy Kiernan had talked. It hadn't been a proper statement, there hadn't been time to take one properly. It hadn't been formally witnessed, nor was it signed. It couldn't be used in any court even if Pallant had wished such a thing. Any competent counsel could tear it to shreds even if it were as much as admissible. But Kiernan had talked before he died and the record, for what it was worth, was in Pallant's safe. It was Jack Pallant's firm intention to keep it there.

Richard Laver had controlled his trembling but was now in the grip of insensate fury. He was a weak man but he wasn't a stupid and all the signals now pointed one way. That mugging had been a put-up job, no mugging at all but protection for Russell.

He began to tick it off reluctantly. The man who had stolen Russell's car had slipped and showed a coloured arm; he had known how to use an anaesthetic which were dangerous in the hands of amateurs. William Wilberforce Smith had been taught how to use them and on top of that he had driven professionally. He was known to worship Charles Russell blindly. How he'd discovered Kiernan's plan (and mine for the matter of that, Laver thought) was something unknown but also irrelevant. Russell had stalled about Willy Smith's voice but of course he would have known it instantly, and Willy wouldn't have taken him violently without giving him an excellent reason. *The* reason, the basic reason. Disaster. For the moment Charles Russell was keeping his mouth shut, unwilling perhaps to foul his own nest, and in any case lacking a shred of proof. And what did that policeman know? He knew *something*. And Russell would now know the lot and that was worse.

It was dangerous at the lowest estimate and all at the door of a single man. His own employee at that.

Intolerable.

For once the veneer of tolerance cracked, the smooth surface of a civilised humanism. What came bursting through was Laver's subconscious, what he'd always tried to suppress and mostly succeeded. He spoke aloud and he snarled as he said it.

"Bloody, bloody, bloody black man."

He had sat for nearly ten minutes in silence, lighting one cigarette from another. He felt as flayed as though he'd been flogged with a sjambok. He had resented what he had seen as impertinence, that a mere policeman should see fit to warn him, and that the cause should be a subordinate, a man whom Charles Russell had unwisely appointed was salt in already festering wounds. His instincts and his service training were both against sudden, decisive action but for once he was going to break free from conditioning. He rang a bell and sent for Willy peremptorily.

Willy came in and was left standing awkwardly. If Laver had wished to ruffle his temper he couldn't have thought of a better way. Damn him, Laver thought – damn all of him. Damn his clothes and his money, that handsome face. Damn him that he adores Charles Russell. Damn him that Russell likes him, too, and can hardly conceal his contempt for me. He said in a voice which Willy had never heard:

"That mugging of Russell."

"Yes, very odd."

"A coloured man did it. The girl saw his arm."

"And since I'm coloured you feel that I owe explanations?" The cool insolence was unexpected and it cut like another blow from the sjambok.

"Where were you that night?"

Willy Smith didn't answer.

"I require an answer."

"Then whistle loudly."

Laver fought for control but didn't regain it; he said in a tone of attempted irony:

"No doubt you can establish an alibi."

Willy said calmly: "Don't be silly."

"What did you say?"

"I said not to be silly."

Laver rose from his chair; he was shaking violently. "You're dismissed," he said. "You will leave at once."

Willy gave him a look which he later remembered, then turned on his heel and went out quietly.

Laver fell back in his chair with a gasp. Fury had sustained him before, now he felt drained to the bottom, an empty man. But not so empty that he didn't feel frightened. After a lifetime of civil service discretion he had just behaved like an ordinary man; he had taken a sudden decision in anger and it could easily be the worst of his life.

Willy collected his few belongings, then went back to his flat and lay down quietly. He was calmer than he had hoped or expected. Laver had lost his head and he hadn't. That was two holes up at the very least but the fact remained he had lost his job. He meant to get it back and quickly though he hadn't an idea how to do it.

11

Willy called next morning on Russell in Ealing. The nursing home was small and homely, one of very few left of a type once common, and he was shown upstairs to Russell's room. Two women were in it already, chattering. They were evidently on excellent terms. One was a stoutish, high-coloured and still attractive, the other as lean as a lath and gently sardonic. The stout one was upbraiding the thin one in an accent from somewhere north of the Border.

"Aggie, you ought to be busted and stripped. Can't you see the wretched man's sweating?"

Aggie walked to the wall and a hanging thermometer. "Nobody sweats at seventeen C."

"Did that come out of some book on nursing?"

"Never mind where it came from. He isn't too hot."

"Not really," Charles Russell said from the bed.

The stoutish lady promptly moved to it; she pulled off a blanket and folded it neatly. The thin one said mildly :

"You can't do that."

"I did a proper job once before I commanded a desk."

Russell made peace and the introductions. "William Wilberforce Smith, an old friend and colleague – Dame Molly Pegg and Sister Agatha. Dame Molly is a friend even older."

"Not happily put."

"I beg your pardon."

Willy bowed politely and waited. Both women gave him that look he had seen before. It had a certain and very proper reserve but it was also the look of a woman's approval. The Dame said :

"Come along, Aggie, they'll want to natter." She took the Sister by the arm and marched her out.

Willy had opened the door and now sat down. Russell was in bed but sitting up. He was a little pale still but otherwise normal. He looked at Willy hard, then said:

"I didn't have time to thank you properly."

"It was nothing. I'm still in your debt."

"Since you feel like that I'll give you good news. You once urged me to go away for a bit and that's exactly what I'm going to do. Dame Molly has rented a seaside villa and has asked me there to convalesce. She was leaving the day you brought me home but came round at once when my housekeeper telephoned. I told you she was a very old friend. Anyway, as soon as she'll let me we'll go down together to Estoril."

"Did you say to Estoril? Where Karel van Loon has a villa too?"

"I'd thought of that, but does it matter?"

"No, I suppose it doesn't really."

Willy Smith was entirely wrong. It was going to matter and matter decisively.

Charles Russell looked at Willy again. "You're not looking well."

"I've had a shock too."

"What sort of shock?"

"I've been given the sack."

Charles Russell sat up straight in bed. "I'm not supposed to smoke but I'm going to. There ought to be one in my jacket pocket."

"There won't be – you smoked your last in that Cortina. But I've brought you one." He produced it unfussily. "Also the sum of nineteen pounds twenty, a wristwatch and a silver lighter."

Russell lit the cigar and for once inhaled it. "Are you telling me these were traced to you and as a consequence you were sacked for stealing?"

"I'm telling you no such thing. I'm not a fool."

"For the second time this morning I beg a pardon." He considered for some time. "Then what happened?"

"It seems that I made a slip with that girl. I didn't notice it then but of course I should have. A sleeve rucked up and she saw my arm. Naturally she mentioned it when it came to telling the police her story. The police must have passed that on to Laver, again naturally since this concerned his predecessor. And Laver knew two other things. The first was that I'd once driven professionally and the second was that I was close to you. So he took a bit of a jump in the dark but he landed on his feet all right. On my feet to be wholly correct."

"What did he do?"

"He called me up. He asked me where I had been that night. He asked me if I could establish an alibi."

"Awkward. And could you?"

"You taught me to be wary of alibis."

"Rightly. And then?"

"I told him to whistle."

"That wasn't diplomatic."

"I know. But in our different ways and for different reasons we were both of us blind, battle angry."

"So he sacked you on the spot?"

"As I literally stood."

Russell said coolly: "I do not blame him." He didn't blame because moral judgments were something he eschewed instinctively, and moreover Richard Laver had had a case. He'd had the case of the man who'd been trapped by emotions, the sort for which psychiatrists had polysyllabic and dubious phrases but which still had their older and simpler nouns. It wasn't in any sense conceited to realise that Laver was jealous of Russell and you had to be very imperceptive indeed not to realise that Laver resented Willy. So the latter confounds your plans for the former. Two critical masses meet and, bang, out comes the mushroom cloud, the flame, the uncontrollable fire of naked hatred. Charles Russell was a logical man and logic demanded a reasonable judgment. In his way he was almost sorry for Laver. He said to William Wilberforce Smith:

"I take it you want your job back?"

"I do."

"You could go to some fancy court or tribunal." It was said with dubiety and Willy brushed it aside.

"And have the Executive pilloried publicly? I couldn't do that and I don't intend to."

For the second time Russell said: "That's my boy." It was the highest commendation he knew. He tapped off his second half inch of ash. "Or I might shuffle around myself a bit. I still know quite a few useful people."

"It's kind of you, sir, but it wouldn't do. I'm not going back because somebody's fixed it – the rest of my time as a placeman, on sufferance. I'm going to *oblige* Richard Laver to take me back."

"You're going to make him eat crow?"

"I'm going to try."

"Dangerous," Russell said. "And unnecessary." He thought carefully before he spoke again. "Richard Laver," he said, "hasn't long to run." He would have agreed with Mrs Phyllis Leech: her husband was very near to the precipice and whatever way he finally fell, whichever way later the politics crumbled, Richard Laver would hardly survive a week. "Apart from what's now the crime of loyalty you've a first-class reputation all round. A new man would almost certainly take you back." Russell felt obliged to say it but he hadn't any serious hope that it would influence William Wilberforce Smith. So he added mildly:

"And have you a plan?"

"I'm afraid I haven't even a glimmer."

Charles Russell put his butt in the ashtray; he appeared to be changing the subject but wasn't. "I believe you have a girlfriend."

"How did you know?"

"I like to keep in touch with my friends' affairs."

"Affair be damned – I intend to marry her. But her father is the old-fashioned sort and he wouldn't let her marry a jobless man."

"So the lady has motive to help you?"

"I hope so."

"May I know her name?"

"Amanda Dee."

"That's pretty."

"Locally she's called the Princess."

"Even prettier. If you pick the right one." The urbane face hadn't changed its expression but it was possible that an eyelid had fluttered. "Where were we?"

"With Amanda Dee."

"Is she sensible?"

"A lot brighter than that."

"Then if I were you I'd tell her everything. Women," Charles Russell continued reflectively, "can often be excessively tiresome but they have advantages which we do not and it's a stupid man who's too proud to use them. They're not hobbled by arbitrary rules of logic; they often see through brick walls clearly while we're picking at the mortar outside them."

Willy seemed to hesitate but Russell waved a hand in dismissal. "Be off with you. Go and talk to Amanda. And if I can ever help you I will. That," he added, for the first time formal, "is an undertaking I mean to honour."

Willy had taken Amanda dancing. He could do this now since a new place had opened, reputable and backed by her father's money. The band played deafening reggae incessantly, but excessive necking was out and so was pot. There was a chucker-out, an ex all-in wrestler, though his services hadn't so far been called on. By the standards of further south-east it was bourgeois; even by local standards it was prim.

But it was a place you could take a princess without risk and Willy had been delighted to do so. They had bounced around like healthy animals, jerking their limbs and clapping loudly. It was as innocent as a nonconformist conference and for the acolytes a lot more fun. Willy had noticed a man he knew, and in one of the rare intervals when the band wasn't beating the customers' brains out he came over to Willy's table and smiled. He said ironically but without offence:

"The great detective."

"You know I'm not that."

Willy introduced Amanda and the other man bowed. "Luiz

Palmer," he said, "and at your service." He pronounced the name the Spanish way.

Willy wasn't anxious for company but he had met this man before and was courteous. "Why don't you join us for a bit?"

"I'd like to but the man I'm with speaks no known tongue but Dutch and some pretty terrible German. He's called Jan and he's pretty good at his job but I doubt if you would find him amusing."

"Then the next time," Willy said.

"With great pleasure."

Luiz's table was out of normal earshot but when he had returned to it Amanda dropped her voice just the same. "Who was that?" she asked. She'd been impressed by his manner.

"He told you his name and I believe it's his real one. He's an Anglo-Argentinian, bilingual in English and Spanish as you'd guess." Willy looked at Amanda and permitted a grin. "But he isn't suitable company for Her Highness Miss Amanda Dee."

"Why ever not?" She sounded faintly resentful.

"Because he's a criminal."

"What?"

"A gangster. I know that's rather an overworked word – I only mean he belongs to a gang. But it's a very high-class organisation. It doesn't go around mugging women."

Unlike myself, he thought, but said nothing.

"Why doesn't the fuzz pick him up?"

"They can't. His organisation is run from England but it hasn't put a foot wrong here. I dare say the Special Branch knows plenty but unless it were just a charge of conspiracy, which all lawyers loathe and policemen more, there isn't a thing in the world they can do."

"Is he the boss?" She was interested and therefore persistent.

"He's not the boss but he's near the top."

"Do you know who the boss is?"

"I once knew him well."

The reggae started again and they went on the floor, dancing themselves into happy exhaustion. Later Willy took her home and this time on the steps she said:

"Father and mother have gone to friends. Why don't you come in?"

"I'd like to do that."

They went into what was still called the parlour, sitting on the sofa and holding hands. The room was vintage turn of the century, the sofa covered in buttoned leather like one of the stuffier clubs in Pall Mall. There was a serving table, now worth a small fortune, and a number of china ornaments beautifully kept. On the walls were late Victorian paintings of huge animals in noble poses and a stuffed owl, under a glass dome, looking knowing. It was anything but fashionable but it was also undeniably comfortable.

Except in the reggae's jungle euphoria he'd been tensed and uneasy for most of the evening, and Amanda who was sensitive as well as being extremely sharp had been tempted to ask him the reason outright. But she had already put a string of questions and there was nothing the ordinary man disliked more than a woman who was over-curious. So she sat on her grandfather's sofa and held Willy's hand. She had hoped for more active entertainment but if he wasn't in the mood she wouldn't tease. She wouldn't tease but she might legitimately stimulate. She said unexpectedly:

"Give me a reefer."

"I never carry them."

"Father uses them on and off when mother's out. I'll see what I can do."

She left the room but returned in three minutes. "Under his handkerchiefs," she said.

"I didn't know you smoked," Willy said.

"This is the fourth in my life."

"Don't get hooked."

"Are you hooked?"

"Not yet. But I do watch it carefully." He blew out a cloud of pungent smoke. "Where did you say you found these things?"

"Under dad's handkerchiefs."

"That's a very old-fashioned place to hide them."

"In his way he's a very old-fashioned man."

The drug had begun to relax him gently; he took another drag and said:

"So old-fashioned that if I lost my job he wouldn't let me marry his daughter."

She had a new string of questions as long as her arm but she wasn't going to risk a banal one. She said simply:

"Tell me the story. I might possibly help."

"That's what Russell advised me to do – come to you."

"Charles Russell?" She was enormously flattered. She had never met Russell but knew Willy adored him. This was an accolade indeed. She said again:

"Willy, tell me the lot."

He did so and she listened in silence, weaving the threads together accurately. When he'd finished she had the story right... Gang is threatening a man called Van Loon with whom Russell had legitimate contacts. But Van Loon's real business is hiding capital and one capitalist fears exposure. If the truth came out it would break his career and he's evidently a powerful man. Sufficiently powerful to order Laver to stop Russell making the mischief he isn't. Willy somehow finds out and saves Russell's life. Laver finds out what he's done and sacks him.

Abominable, she thought. Contemptible. Her Willy had done the only thing possible.

"I know you don't drink but I need one badly."

She went to the sideboard and poured one thoughtfully from a decanter of fine Irish glass. Surprisingly it was gin and water, not the normal drink of a well-born young lady. She returned to the sofa and took a long swig at it. She could see that Willy was slowly relaxing – telling the tale had done him good. But she mustn't rush her fences and scare him nor give the impression of cross-examining. She'd have to lead him to her own conclusion, not beat at the wall of masculine obstinacy.

"That gangster we met in the club tonight. Is he part of the gang which is after Van Loon?"

"His lot works mainly in South America."

"But he did have a Dutchman with him. He told us."

"That could be a coincidence."

"Which I thought you'd been taught you should always mistrust."

He thought it over and Amanda Dee watched him. She could almost hear the male mind grinding. To herself it had been simple and clear: this had been a gift from the gods and only a man would think of doubting it. He said at length:

"All right. Go on."

She knew exactly what she wanted to say but she couldn't just slap it down on the table – he'd shy away. She must feed it to him in separate courses.

"How does extortion really operate?"

He could answer this and did so coolly. By now he had relaxed completely. "By blackmail if you've got something to go on but this lot mostly goes for kidnapping. They snatch a man and hold him to ransom. As often as not they also get it."

"It sounds dangerous," she said.

"It is. The essence of a successful kidnapping is to keep the affair as private as possible. If your hideout is discovered you're in trouble. There'll be policemen all round and in some countries soldiers. The Press and the cameras – negotiation in public. In effect you'll be under a sort of siege."

She planted the first *banderilla* neatly. "I should have thought there was an easier way."

"Such as what?"

"Such as going for the money directly."

He understood her but shook his head at once. She was irritated and poured more gin to hide it. Men were creatures of unshakeable habit. They did a thing one way all their lives and to get them to change it was next to impossible. So she wouldn't return to that road directly: instead she'd make it seem the idea was his own.

"You told me Van Loon was running for Portugal."

"I told you that that's what Charles Russell advised him."

"He'd hardly have gone to Russell at all if he hadn't been willing to take his advice."

He nodded; he accepted that.

"And if he runs at all he'll hardly go penniless."

She could see that he'd begun to think seriously. "Would you like some coffee?"

"Thanks. Very much."

She went into the kitchen to make it and when she came back his mood had changed. He was out of his depression now, asking the questions and asking them eagerly.

"What exactly are you suggesting? Lay it down."

But she had one more question herself and asked it. "How well do you know the head of this gang?"

"I haven't seen him for quite some time but we were friends at school and I once did him a service."

Secretly, she applauded loudly. This was better than she had dared to hope. But he had returned to his own question firmly.

"You've been cooking something besides this coffee. I want to know what it is."

. . . I've nearly got him.

She said with a measured hint of formality: "I think you should go to this school friend of yours and make him a business proposition. He's to lay off any idea of ransom and you'll help him in a straightforward robbery."

"And what do we get out of that?"

"Your job back."

"How?"

She told him with the simple precision of a woman who knew her mind exactly. For three or four seconds he looked blank as a wall, then he called upon a God long forgotten.

"It should be you in the Executive, not me."

She saw that she had him now and struck. "With his account books you could make your own terms. The names would be political dynamite."

"Supposing he hasn't brought them with him?"

"Would he dare leave them behind in Holland? Would you if you were doing what he is?"

"No, I suppose I wouldn't. That's right. But I might think that they were better destroyed."

"*You* might. But you're not a Dutch banker."

"It isn't watertight," he said at last.

"Then have you a better idea?"

"No, none."

"I know it's a bit of a gamble," she said.

He laughed again. "Have you ever met Russell?"

"No, never. Why?"

"Sometimes you sound exactly like him."

"That's the nicest thing you've ever said to me."

He pulled her off the sofa and kissed her. "That must do for tonight but it's on account. I've got to get up early tomorrow."

"Damn getting up early tomorrow."

"So be it."

Half an hour later he took his leave. Amanda Dee was crying quietly but he could see that her tears were not of grief. "I'll get up early tomorrow anyway. My friend lives in Wiltshire. It's quite a drive."

12

But not so far that he need rise before ten, and for that mercy he
was properly grateful. Willy threaded his car through the maze
of Salisbury, then at Wilton turned left for the meadows and
chalk streams. This was fisherman's country and he had been
here before. Charles Russell had brought him one day to watch,
for he believed in sharing pleasures with friends. But Willy had
decided quickly that fishing with dry fly was not his sport. He
could appreciate the enormous skills, the even more enormous
patience, but he thought the affair was over-conventionalised. A
worm on a hook caught as many fish, and if it was food you were
after, not sport, a well-laid seine caught even more. But he had
kept these heretical thoughts to himself. Charles Russell would
have thought them barbarous.

He drove to his village and stopped on the bridge. Two miles
upstream was a well-known fishing club where Russell often
rented a room. Below him the water ran smooth and clear, kept
free of too much weed and all debris. Russell had told him that
that was expensive but that left to itself a stream choked in two
summers. Now it ran silently, away to eternity. It was the stuff
of a superior elegy but Willy was here on business, not to muse.

He drove to the village: it hadn't changed. There was a cluster
of ancient elegant cottages, a post office cum village shop, a church
whose priest now covered several, and beside it an unpretentious
manor. Willy drove to it and rang the bell.

A maid opened and for a moment stared. Men of colour were
a rarity here. But she had the countrywoman's natural good
manners and the stare soon changed to a friendly smile. She knew

without having to ask the question that Willy wasn't selling insurance.

"Is Mr Armitage in?"

"I think so, sir. Please come in while I go and see."

She showed him into the study and left him, and Willy looked round in appreciation. The furniture was a good deal older than that of the room where he'd talked to Amanda but had the same quiet air of solid comfort. On the walls were several pictures, well lighted. Willy had little knowledge of painting but an instinctive feeling for what was good. Whoever, over the generations, had commissioned these portraits or bought these landscapes had known what he was doing perfectly.

A man came in in a tattered pullover. Perhaps he was a year older than Willy but like Willy he looked in excellent shape. He too for a moment stared, then laughed; he held out his hand.

"Why, Willy Smith! It's been too long."

"I won't pretend I was simply passing. I've come to ask for help."

"It is yours."

Dick Armitage spoke the words sincerely. They'd been at school together and Willy had lied for him. Lied like a gentleman, Armitage thought. If he hadn't he himself would have been out. As it was they could still play club cricket together.

He rang the bell for an elderly manservant. "Last time we met we were playing Lord's ground staff. I remember that you didn't drink."

"This is a special occasion."

"Then sherry? And of course you will stay to lunch."

"I'd like to."

The weather had turned unseasonably chilly and they settled in chairs by a brisk fire of logs. Dick Armitage said:

"Now what's the trouble?"

Willy was grateful for the other's directness. He hadn't Amanda Dee's techniques and preferred to ride his fences straight.

"Then to start with I know what you really do."

"Indeed?" It was spoken without the least resentment and also without a hint of embarrassment. "I imagine that if anyone does it would be you and your Security Executive."

"From which I have just had the sack. But that comes later."

"Increasingly interesting – please go on. But before you do let me clear the decks. My ostensible business is a chain of cycle shops which my grandfather founded and have since flourished mightily. Behind that, as you appear to know, I run something which is rather different. I suppose I must reluctantly call it a gang since 'organisation' sounds horribly pompous and 'group' suggests yobbos with electric guitars. We specialise in extortion by kidnapping but we're not the sort of people we're sometimes thought." The tone changed to unconcealed contempt. "Urban guerrillas and half-baked anarchists – I wouldn't give one a job as a driver. Our interest is in money, not politics, and we make quite a lot of it fairly successfully. So if you've come to me for work I might fit you in but I thought it fair to give you the background. If you've any urge to save the world, any leaning to the Lunatic Left, I'm afraid you're not the type I could use."

"I haven't come for a job."

"Then what?"

"A deal."

"What sort of a deal?"

"I'll try and tell you."

Willy Smith collected his thoughts: a mistake was going to be instantly fatal. "You operate mostly in South America."

"That is correct." He was still unembarrassed.

"Where Luiz is no doubt very useful."

"I didn't know you knew him."

"Not well. I met him twice before you recruited him and last night I went to a club with my girl. He came over and wished us both good evening."

"Luiz prides himself on *hidalgo* manners."

Willy knew he was approaching his crisis: his next sentence might see him thrown out on his ear. He drew a deep breath and said deliberately:

"He also had a Dutchman with him."

For a moment Armitage seemed to hesitate, then he shrugged and said coolly:

"That would be Jan. Jan is an inside man and a good one. We slipped him into a house in Holland and he once did a frightening-job with a gun. Now he's here lying low with Luiz till we're ready for the serious business." Dick Armitage threw a log on the fire. When he turned he said quietly: "Your guess is right. I *am* planning an operation in Holland and I'm breaking my own rules by doing so. Karel van Loon, since you know so much, is a very rich man and we'll show a profit but I also want to square private accounts and that's bang against the rules of sound business. Did you know I was partly Dutch?"

"Why should I?"

"In fact it was my maternal grandmother. She was a widow and when the Germans came in she got her only daughter to England where, as things turned out, she married my father. But she herself was deep in the Underground and later had to go into hiding. Van Loon betrayed her hiding place and the family which was doing the hiding. She died in a work-camp, a pitiful skeleton. And she was only one of many hundreds. The Gestapo paid Karel van Loon in cash or sometimes by a looted picture. He has a famous Vermeer which the old man would tell you was nothing but a very good copy. Perhaps he knew and perhaps he didn't. But Karel van Loon knows it isn't a copy. There was an Inquisition about looted pictures but quite a few are still unaccounted for. Perhaps they got burnt in Berlin or re-looted. In any case this Vermeer is the real one. But it isn't the picture I want; I want Van Loon. I don't mean to kill him, he'll die one day anyway, but a penniless Van Loon will suffer. I must confess that's a thought I greatly relish." Dick Armitage smiled but not in amusement. "So you see I am mixing business with pleasure and that's always a foolish thing to do."

A gong sounded and they went into lunch, a single dish well cooked, then cheese. Afterwards they returned to the study. The meal gave Willy time to reflect for Armitage's story had tangled his thinking. But he decided that it hadn't changed it. Armitage had two motives, not one, and Willy, if he were skilful, might use both.

At lunch they had talked of indifferent matters, of schooldays and common friends and cricket tours, and it was Armitage who after it came back to the matter in hand directly.

"You said you had lost your job – I don't ask why. But I meant it when I said I could fit you in."

"It's kind of you but I want my own job back."

"And how are you going to do that?"

"Will you listen?"

"That means it's probably quite outrageous."

"It is and it also needs your help. In return for that you might see an advantage. That's what I meant when I talked of a deal."

"I'm a business man when I'm not being foolish."

"Then when are you going to grab Van Loon?"

"Within the next three days or never. Van Loon is going to run for Portugal – a hideout called Villa Fleury at Estoril. Jan has reported he's sold his gold and I dare say he's sent his bearers ahead of him but they'll still be held to his order somewhere and Luiz can be very persuasive."

"And the Vermeer?"

"Jan believes it's still in Holland. He means to take it with him when he runs."

"Why not let him go clear and increase the stake?"

Dick Armitage shook his head to that. "Because I couldn't snatch him in Portugal. A snatch needs careful organisation and if you don't know the local mores and haven't friends the snags increase by three or four fold."

"I wasn't suggesting you snatch Van Loon."

"Then what *were* you suggesting?"

"To go directly for the collected loot. The bearers may be in a bank for a bit but he won't dare leave them there for long, a target for international trouble. He'll cache them in his house when he's ready and the house will also hold the Vermeer. You talked about how he would suffer poor, but Van Loon will never be really penniless so long as he keeps a famous picture. So I'm suggesting you go and lift the lot."

Dick Armitage laughed but at once apologised. "I was laughing at myself, not at you. It's deplorable how one-tracked one gets. I've been making a living snatching bodies and I've simply never thought about snatching things. But I do have one or two questions."

"Shoot."

"If he keeps his stuff at home he'll keep it well. Some millions of pounds-worth of bearer bonds isn't something you put under the mattress. There'll be a very good safe, perhaps even a strong room, and though I've a well-trained, disciplined outfit not one is any sort of peterman."

"We're not going to need a peterman."

"No?" Dick Armitage had noted the plural but let it pass.

"Karel van Loon will open things for us. Luiz, as you remarked, will persuade him."

"No doubt of that but how to get in? The house may be a minor fortress and again I've got nobody good at that line."

"We go through the front door without nonsense."

"And how do we manage that?"

"I've a friend."

Dick Armitage stared at Willy hard. "If you want me to take what you're saying seriously you've got to do better than just 'a friend'."

"He's called Colonel Charles Russell."

"The man who recruited you? The late head of the Security Executive? He'd help you in what's clearly a crime?"

"I told you I had just lost my job there. I lost it because I did Russell a service. If you press me that service was saving his life."

Dick Armitage was seriously interested. The complex of motives, debts owed and to pay, was a Medusa web of fascination. But there was one loose end, Willy Smith's own advantage.

"You can tell me if you want to later what happened between yourself and the Executive but for the moment I must know one thing. He was suddenly as hard as steel. *What do you get yourself from this?*"

"I mean to get my job back."

"How?"

"I'm gambling that that safe of Van Loon's holds more than just cash and bearer bonds. I'm gambling it holds his private ledgers, and if the names in those are what I believe them, I can get my job back just by saying I've got them."

Dick Armitage started to laugh but checked himself. "A classic," he said admiringly. "Beautiful." He took another moment off to think. The plan had an attractive simplicity, the logic of the good criminal mind. He wondered where in fact it had come from. William Wilberforce Smith was undeniably smart but he didn't believe he had cooked up this one. Dick Armitage had made plans himself and had criticised the plans of others. Each bore its author's thumbprint indelibly, the painstaking, the apparently brilliant, the one which fell to pieces in your hand. The essential was a clear objective.

Women were very good at that. They might not be quite so hot on the detail but show them three doors at the end of a passage and invariably they picked the right one.

Dick Armitage was almost sold but he had one more question and asked it simply.

"Just how does your Russell get us in?"

"He has met Van Loon more than once, quite innocently. Van Loon has this house at Estoril and Russell is there too at this moment. I told you I saved his life and I did but in the process he hit his head on a windscreen. So he's down at Estoril convalescing, in the villa of an old flame called Pegg. He can fix it to meet Van Loon again naturally and after that he has great resource."

"So I have heard. And when he gets in, I presume fairly legally, we shall be just behind him – less so?"

Willy nodded and Armitage thought again. "I'll tell you what I'll do," he said finally. "I won't scrub the operation in Holland but I'm ready to postpone it a bit. I can't do that for very long because once Van Loon is out of Holland I lose the option of simply snatching him. So you must make your reconnaissance and fix it with Russell and you must do it within forty-eight hours."

"I'll leave tonight."

"I can see you mean business. If you come back to me with

good flesh on the bones I'll seriously consider your plan. For the moment I won't go further than that. You talked about gambles and I'm a gambler. But I play the odds or I wouldn't be here. I think you understand me."

"Perfectly."

Armitage had been sipping port wine but now he unexpectedly rose. He threw the last of the wine in the fire and laughed. It wasn't enough to put it out but the steam curled up the great chimney ritually.

"A libation to the old gods we've forgotten."

It had been a very bad twenty-four hours for Karel van Loon. He had been telephoning to his agent daily and had been promised that work on the villa would finish – within three days, then five, and now three more again. And his talk with Russell had not been emollient, for Russell had taken his problem seriously. Go away and lie low, he had said, or else.

Karel van Loon couldn't wait to run.

The first event to shake him further was a letter in his office that morning. It was the report on Jan from his firm of enquiry agents. Jan was indeed a trained male nurse, a trade he had learnt in Indonesia before returning to Holland where his father had taken him, fleeing for his life from Hitler's Reich. He hadn't been a Jew, just a Liberal, but he'd been a thorn in the flesh of the Reich's authorities, and later, during the Occupation, he had had to go into hiding with the rest. But he'd been sufficiently tiresome for the Gestapo to go after him and it appeared he had been coldly betrayed. He had died under interrogation. It was believed the son was now in England and that aspect was being pursued with vigour.

Karel van Loon had disliked this news since the suggestion of motive was naggingly sinister. But it wasn't enough alone to panic him. He already suspected that Jan had been planted, and after all, he told himself, he hadn't been the only delator. There had been other collaborators who had betrayed men in hiding, be- trayed for money or food or a looted valuable. Like Charles

Russell he mistrusted coincidence and he could tell himself no connection was proven. He tried to put it aside and partly succeeded.

But in the evening the second blow fell from the sky. He had taken a taxi home from his office and somewhere it had turned left, not right. Van Loon had been trying to snatch a nap for the strain of the last few days had drained him. When he noticed they had gone wrong he panicked. So this was the orthodox snatch by taxi. It had all been absurdly easy. They'd got him.

He was shivering as he fought for control. At last he tapped the taxi-man's shoulder.

"Driver!"

Van Loon had not expected an answer but the driver said politely: "Yes sir?"

"This isn't the way to my house."

"I'm sorry." The driver pulled up to the kerb at once. "I'm new to Amsterdam," he said.

Van Loon fell back in his seat, exhausted. He could barely find words to give directions.

But later as he struggled to sleep he realised that the man had been lying. There were very strict exams for taxi-drivers, it was impossible he had lost his way in a popular quarter of Amsterdam. It had been cruelly well calculated, wholly sadistic. First terror and then relief. Then fear again, an increasing fear.

At three in the morning he got up to make tea. His pyjamas were soaked but he changed them reluctantly. It wasn't the day for changing pyjamas and Karel van Loon was inescapably mean.

When dawn came he was shivering again for like Laver he'd had to face a truth. The Commissaris had already guessed it but Van Loon had recoiled from the basilisk face. This couldn't be just an abduction for money, the build-up had been too long and too cruel. They were playing cat and mouse with him, they were out for revenge as well as money. He cursed the Portuguese comprehensively, their dilatoriness, their too easy promises, at bottom their unbreakable stubbornness. Everything was ready but the house, the Villa Fleury. The last of the bearer bonds had gone to its temporary home in a Portuguese bank, the Vermeer had been deframed and packed, and he would take it on his final run in the car which he kept at Red Alert.

The killer came next morning by hand, a further report from his private eyes. Jan, the male nurse, was indeed in England and in contact with a man called Armitage. Armitage was a business man but secretly financed extortion. The British police were unable to touch him since he had never put a foot wrong in England. He was also half Dutch on his mother's side and it was believed that his grandmother had been betrayed to the Gestapo.

Van Loon fought himself but reached for the telephone. It was the fourth time he had rung in thirty-six hours. His agent's bland voice held no hint of urgency. No, unhappily it was still raining hard and serious building (the voice emphasised 'serious') was out of the question as long as it did so. But the weather forecast suggested improvement and perhaps by sometime next week . . .

Van Loon got the phone on its slot but only just.

13

Willy Smith arrived in Portugal by a shabby flight from a shabby airport but he had been given forty-eight hours and couldn't choose. It was four o'clock in the morning and chilly, and he was grateful he'd brought a lightweight overcoat. He dozed for a couple of hours in a chair, then shaved and drank a cup of coffee. He found a taxi which took him to Estoril.

He told it to stop at the Monte station for he had had time to do his simple homework and knew where the Villa Fleury was. But he didn't wish to attract attention so he paid off the taxi and started to walk. Once across the main road and the tatty park the ground began to rise fairly steeply. The area was a trifle seedy but had once been very grand indeed. There were fine houses along the road at the crest, and one or two were still well kept on sites which overlooked the sea. Willy found the Villa Fleury and stopped to goggle, recognising the style at once. It was bastard Loire château and not his favourite. There was a lodge at the entrance but nobody in it. Willy walked in and was immediately challenged.

The man who did so was much darker than Willy with a fleshier nose and fuller lips. Willy touched his cap politely.

"I'm sorry I can't speak Portuguese."

The man answered him in excellent English. "A West Indian, are you? I think you've been lucky. I'm an Angolan and I haven't been lucky." He stared at Willy who didn't flinch. "What are you doing here?"

"Taking a walk." He looked as though he were taking a walk. He had a cap and a stick and his stoutest shoes. His overcoat he had left at the airport. He said casually: "You speak very good English."

"I'm a Bachelor of Science of the University of Cambridge." He wore overalls and dusty boots. Willy looked at his hands: they had started to callouse. The man caught the glance and said unsmiling:

"My father was an engineer and I was to inherit the business. It was mostly with the Angolan whites so when the commies took over we were naturally suspect. To my father they gave some farcical trial but he always knew they would end by shooting him. Me they let go at the price of the business. So here I am with thousands of others but those others are mostly whites. I am black. For months I had no work at all, or working on the roads as a labourer, but now I'm a sort of contractor's foreman." He managed a crooked smile and added: "I said I hadn't been lucky but I have."

"I'm sorry," Willy said.

"Oh hell! At least I get a regular wage, and for a building job this one is interesting."

The man seemed eager to talk and Willy let him. "Really?" he said. He managed it perfectly. He didn't sound too interested but made it clear he was ready to listen.

"I'd show you round if it wouldn't cost me my job but I reckon the man we're doing this for is some sort of international crook."

Some surprise was now permissible. "What?"

"Who else but a crook would want a strongroom? That's what the cellar is now – a vault. Modern safe and all the trimmings. Electrified." He waved at the tall old hedge round the garden. "That's electrified too. And down by the lodge we'll be fitting a fancy gate. The lodgekeeper will be able to open it and so will the man in the house. If he wants to." *l*

"It certainly smells of something to hide."

"I can see you've lived in England a long time."

They shook hands and Willy went on his way. He hadn't hoped for a really close inspection but had learnt the basic layout without one. He took out his map and read it carefully. He was making for Dame Molly's villa and for Russell who was convalescing there.

She let him in herself and smiled. "I remember you – you came to Ealing. So you've come again." She waved behind her. "He's out by the pool. Forgive me if I go on cooking. Just go through the sitting room and down the steps from the terrace."

She bustled away and Willy followed her gesture. The garden was large, in the Latin manner – few flowers and poor grass but a well-kept *parterre*. At the bottom was a substantial pool and Russell was sitting by it, reading. He looked up at Willy's foot-steps.

"Why Willy!" He was about to offer a conventional greeting but checked himself, looking hard at Willy. "You're looking very serious."

"Yes, I am."

"Then bring a chair from the pavilion, please, and another gin and tonic for me."

Willy brought both and Russell thanked him. "I'm afraid this is going to take some time." It would, he thought – Amanda and Armitage, why he was here and what he hoped from it.

"I've all the time in the world. Tell your story."

Willy did so and Russell listened in silence. He seldom moved his eyes from Willy's face. He had an almost feminine sensitivity and was reading the least change of expression. At the end of twenty minutes he said:

"I like it. It's neat."

"I suppose you wouldn't help to pull it off."

"I told you I'd help you to get your job back." There was the faintest hint of irritation.

"I didn't mean to doubt your word."

"Then stop havering and tell me how."

"Could you get us into that house?"

"I might. When do you want to do this thing?"

"As soon as possible after Van Loon's arrival."

"Of which you will naturally keep me informed."

"Certainly. No problem there."

Charles Russell finished his drink reflectively. "Two questions," he said, "but only two. Are you sure that Vermeer is really genuine?"

"Armitage says so. He knows it provenance."

"And that it was payment for selling people in hiding?"

"Armitage is half Dutch. They're a people who don't forget things easily."

Charles Russell relapsed into frozen silence. He was thinking he'd never liked Van Loon and at the time had been mildly ashamed of the prejudice. And now instinct had been abundantly justified. Delators were his unfavourite people. The boy who sneaked at school, the crook who grassed – they were nothing against a man like Van Loon. He remembered the splendid picture and shuddered. Forced labour, he thought, and starvation. Torture and death. The old masterpiece now stank of blood.

When he spoke again his voice had hardened. "I'll get you in there if I can, Willy Smith, but nothing in this world is certain. I would put it at a hundred to eight."

"Having worked for you I'd call that cramping the odds."

"Well there it is – you can tell Mr Armitage. But I'm making a single and simple condition. If I get you inside I'm coming too."

"I will put that to Armitage."

"No you will not." The voice was now that of a man in his prime, the head of the Security Executive. "You will state it as a condition precedent and your own interest is that your friend accepts it. I'm afraid it's as simple as that."

"I'll do it just the way you say."

Willy returned by a less barbarous flight, even snatching a few hours in his bed. He felt he had earned them but rose early next morning. Armitage had said forty-eight hours and he wasn't a man to extend a deadline.

Willy found him eating an English breakfast and accepted the invitation to join him. He hadn't eaten a proper meal for longer than he cared to remember, and though he had had a few hours sleep he felt tired and more than a little jaded.

"You're looking pretty knackered," Armitage said.

"It's showing, is it? But on the whole it's been worth it. I saw the house and I talked to Russell."

"Start on the house."

Willy Smith reported shortly and Armitage used a word he'd used before. "A fortress," he said. *Festung Van Loon.* You were lucky with that unhappy Angolan. Later I'll show our appreciation."

"I'm sure he'd be very grateful for that."

"And Russell?"

"He confirmed he would keep his promise to help me."

"More precisely, please."

"By getting us inside the fortress. I say 'us' because I'd like to come too."

"That I had assumed already." Armitage was detached but friendly. "Did he say how?"

"I didn't ask him."

"I know him only by hearsay but you were wise."

"But he offered a hundred to eight on success."

"That's good enough for me. I'll take it."

The difficult part was coming now and Willy took a deliberate breath. "But he also made one firm condition."

"Did he indeed? And what was that?"

"That if he got us inside he was going to come too."

To Willy's surprise there was instant agreement. "I understand his feelings perfectly since they're not so very different from my own. I'm suffering from Staff Officer's Sickness. I've been sitting behind a desk for too long, planning what other men do successfully, and if you do that for too long you go mad. Worse, you begin to feel infallible and that's the most fatal feeling a man can have. The only known cure is to see some action so I'd already decided to come on this trip. And if I go why shouldn't Colonel Charles Russell? He's led a vigorous and varied life and I dare say he's feeling a trifle bored. In any case I'll accept him with pleasure."

"He won't be any use if there's rough stuff."

"I wouldn't take him along for the rough stuff. But if a half of what I hear is a quarter true he can still think like lightning, and in the pinches, if there are any, that can be very useful indeed. The very best sort of ally – an equal." Dick Armitage started to think aloud. "As I see it five men should be quite enough – yourself and Russell, myself and Luiz, plus Jan to drive and keep watch while we're inside. He may not have Luiz Palmer's intelligence but he's a well-trained, wholly reliable operator. Luiz I'll send ahead at once since there are things we shall need to know before pulling the switch." Armitage ticked them off on his fingers. "Most obvious the date of Van Loon's arrival, then confirmation that he has moved his loot from wherever he had temporarily cached it. Thirdly, his domestic arrangements – do servants sleep in and are there dogs? There'll be a man in the gatehouse and I'm afraid he'll get hurt but I'm a softie about killing animals. Finally Luiz will contact Russell and tell him when we're ready to move. As soon as I hear that Van Loon has arrived I'll go down myself for the detailed arrangements. If you'd like to come with me I've no objections."

"I'd like to very much."

"Very well, that's settled. And I'd be grateful for a second head since all this is going to need careful timing. If we strike too soon without proper staff work we could easily screw the whole thing up, and if we give Van Loon too much time to settle it's conceivable he could make it more difficult. Leave me your telephone number. I'll call you."

Willy drove back to London elated. He could tell a first-class plan when he saw one.

Van Loon was at the extreme of tension when the news came through that the villa was ready. Several times he had almost run for it – house or no house he must end the agony – but reason had in the end restrained him. In an undefended house he'd be vulnerable not only to well-organised gangs but to any little local criminal who happened to learn or suspect the position. So somehow he had reined himself, but when the news came at last he had left in an hour.

Now he had the reward of self-discipline, walking round the garden quietly. The splendid high hedge almost hid the house and entirely hid the wire fence inside it. That could and would be turned on at night. By day the gate was controlled from the gatehouse but at night it could be switched to his bedroom. The front door was always his – he was living alone. Two women came in at different times to clean and do his simple cooking but from six he was the king of the castle.

A fine one, he thought, as he went indoors. One of the women served his luncheon. He hadn't eaten well for some time but now he began to eat with relish . . . By God, he had made it, he really had. He'd have to keep his head well down for a year at least and maybe more but he wasn't deeply dependent on social life. Then perhaps if all went well he might join the club. There was golf there and tennis and presumably bridge, and later he'd think of loosening further. Meanwhile he would read and learn the language. He was there for the rest of his life so he'd have to.

When he'd finished his lunch he inspected the house. He had done it before but it gave him pleasure. Every window was grilled with electric alarms which rang both in the gatehouse and also his bedroom. At night he slept with a loaded gun but his real defences were located elsewhere. He checked them with a satisfied smile. Steep steps ran down to the strongroom's door and inside was a large and expensive safe. Both were controlled from hidden switches, for a bank in Amsterdam had been broken, its elaborate combinations proved useless. So safebreakers were clever nowadays but there was a third switch which would discourage one finally.

Van Loon went back to his study still smiling. He said aloud what he'd thought before :

"By God, I've made it. I really have."

He should have poured some wine on the floor as he uttered it.

Luiz Palmer had called on Charles Russell before but only to introduce himself, to explain why he was there at all, but this morning he had come with hard news. He shook hands in the continental manner and when Russell asked him to sit brought a chair. "I've been busy," he said.

"I'm sure you have." Russell was speaking no more than the

truth. Luiz Palmer did not look a laggard. He was tall and wiry with dark hair but fair skin. His English and Latin blood had blended well.

"Van Loon arrived three days ago and a security van drove up the day after. I think we may assume it contained his loot."

"Which he'd had to put in a bank until ready?" Russell answered his own question. "Yes. Go on."

"Then besides what we learnt from Willy Smith I've done a little on the domestic details. Van Loon is living very quietly. There's a man in the lodge but no one sleeps in. The second daily woman leaves at six. Mr Armitage and Willy Smith arrived as soon as I'd told them Van Loon had. The Dutchman arrived this morning by air. That makes a full muster – all we need."

"Except to get in."

"Which we left to you with every confidence."

"I hope it wasn't misplaced. I hate messes." Russell reflected but simply said: "When?"

"We should like to move tomorrow evening. There'll be a conference in the afternoon first."

"In this climate I sleep in the afternoon."

Luiz Palmer took it without a blink. "Then the conference will be changed to the morning. May I ask a question?"

"Yes, of course."

"Have you contacted Van Loon yet?"

"No, not yet. But on what you now tell me I'll do it at once." He rose and they walked back to the house. Luiz Palmer asked:

"You will no doubt confirm?"

"I've done some planning myself, you know."

"I'm sure you have, sir." Luiz bowed and departed.

Russell went to the study and used the telephone. Like Luiz he hadn't been wholly idle, and although Van Loon's number was ex-directory a surprisingly small sum of money had bought it. He dialled and a cautious voice said:

"Who is it?"

"Charles Russell here."

There were several seconds of total silence, silence which spelt success or failure. If Van Loon rang off Russell's plan was off too, but Russell didn't think he would. In Van Loon's place he would have seen this call against the background of what had passed between them. Either it was innocent, in which case to ring off would look odd; it might even cause Russell to start enquiries and at the moment any enquiry was dangerous. Alternatively the call had significance and in that case it would be wise to learn it.

The seconds ticked by and Russell waited. Finally Van Loon said neutrally:

"I didn't know you were down here too."

Charles Russell let his breath out quietly; he was inside the Villa Fleury now but he wasn't going to spoil his hand by playing out his winners too early.

"I had a little accident and I'm staying with a friend to recover."

"I'm sorry to hear it."

"It's nothing really. I thought it might be nice to meet again."

"I'm living very quietly."

"*I know.*"

First high card down. Let's see how he takes it.

He took it without an audible flinch. "I see you have an excellent memory."

"I can remember why you asked me to help you."

The manner sharpened into a sudden anxiety. "Has something gone wrong?"

"From your point of view you could certainly say so."

"If you could give me some idea – "

"Your Vermeer."

"Oh that. It's a copy."

"*So I have heard.*"

. . . Naturally he'll think it's blackmail and in one sense it very surely is.

There was another long pause but when it ended Karel van Loon was brisk and businesslike. "You are interested in my Vermeer?"

"Very interested."

"In that case I'm prepared to discuss it."

"I think you would be wise to do so."

"And *I* think I understand you perfectly. At what time do you propose to call?"

"Tomorrow evening at half-past six?"

"That will be convenient. Now listen carefully. Ring the bell on the outside gate and a man will open it. Then walk to the front door and ring again. Ring two short and two long for identification. I will release the lock. Come straight in. My study is the first on the left. I shall be ready to receive you."

No doubt.

Charles Russell went to his room and changed, then out to the pleasant veranda to think. Dame Molly found him there half an hour later. She started on some casual pleasantry but suddenly checked it and looked at him hard.

"Charles, you're planning some mischief."

"Yes." She was a woman and they were very old friends. It would be useless to try to deceive her – she'd spot it. Come to think of it he didn't wish to.

"Dangerous mischief?"

"I very much hope not."

"Why get involved?"

"I owe a debt."

She knew that was final but tried again. "I don't want the bother of shipping your body home."

"Or of writing my epitaph."

"Would I have to do that too?"

"Yes, but it's already decided. We decided it in my club one night. 'There's another bottle coming' – remember?"

She managed a wan smile. "I do. But I also remember you weren't in a hurry for it."

14

Dick Armitage, Luiz and Willy Smith were staying at the same hotel, Jan at another where the owner spoke Dutch. Armitage had a modest sitting room and there the meeting was held next morning.

For once Charles Russell arrived five minutes late, apologising for a defaulting taxi. Willy Smith introduced him to Armitage gracefully and they all sat down on chairs round a table. Armitage sat on the chair at its head, a single sheet of paper before him. He was formally dressed in a suit and a tie, and Russell noticed it was the same as Willy's. "Gentlemen," he said, "to business." He sounded confident and entirely unfussy. Russell recognised the manner easily, that of the good general in conference. Not the foxy type nor the barking dog, not the sort which was there on some Prime Minister's whim and gave embarrassing pep talks to private soldiers. On the contrary the strict professional who would listen to suggestions gladly provided that they too were professional. Colonel Charles Russell felt comfortably at home.

Armitage turned to him first and Russell nodded. "As I've already confirmed to Luiz Palmer I have an appointment with Van Loon at half-past six. The gateman will open the outside gate and I'm to ring the front door bell in two short and two long. His study is the first room on the left. I shall try to distract the gateman as I go through."

Dick Armitage nodded in turn. "When Jan will take him. He isn't here because he doesn't speak English but Luiz will give him his orders in German. How are you going to go to the villa?"

"I thought on foot would be simplest."

"I quite agree. So we four will be behind in the station wagon.

When you reach the gate we'll drive past you and stop – the gatehouse faces the opposite way. The moment the gate moves so will Jan. He'll be told not to kill but he will disable. Then he'll go back to the wagon and keep watch. Any questions, please?"

"So far none."

"Then phase two begins with ourselves inside the gate. We walk to the door and Russell rings as instructed. Van Loon releases the door and we all go in." So far he had been talking generally but now he looked at Russell directly. "Do you think he will be armed?"

"I can only say that in his place I wouldn't be. He believes I am coming to blackmail him, not to rob, and against blackmailers guns are a very poor argument. Besides, if he has one he would hardly dare use it. The last thing he'll want in a strange foreign country is a body to be explained away."

"Nevertheless it's still a risk." Armitage turned his head to Luiz but Luiz gave his most Latin shrug. "I've disarmed an armed man before now," he said, "but I don't want you to think I'm boasting. It can really be surprisingly easy provided the gun can't fire a burst. Especially when there are others present. One of them makes a sudden distraction . . ." He waved a hand and went back to silence.

"So anything on phase two?"

There was not.

"So regarded as planning phase three is the weakest since most of it must be played by ear. We're agreed that our only chance of success is to oblige Van Loon to open up for us, but how long that will take I do not know." Armitage returned to Russell. "You know him best. Would you say he was brave?"

"Not brave. But he's the type to turn desperate."

"He won't have time to do that," Luiz said. He showed small and very white teeth as he said it.

"Then I don't think we can carry that further. As I said, we'll have to play them as they fall. As for phase four, the getaway, that has been fairly straightforward detail. I've a fast cabin cruiser moored in the Tagus with a couple of men of my own to man her. To Casablanca is roughly five hundred miles and the gateman won't be discovered till morning when the first of the daily maids comes in. The cruiser can make twenty knots, a little more if you really push her, and in ten hours we'll be comfortably out of range of anything but an aircraft sent after us. And candidly I think that's unlikely."

"And once in Casablanca?" Willy asked.

"Have you ever been there?"

"Never."

"I know it well. I have powerful connections there, and even if I didn't have friends a couple of million pounds in bearers can buy you a great deal of help in Morocco. We'll lie low for a bit and then drift home separately. That's myself and Luiz and also Jan. Van Loon will have to report he's been robbed – he could hardly accept the risks of not doing so – and he'll be able to give some description of Luiz and me. But he has neither met us nor knows our names." Armitage added a trifle drily: "And I do not propose to make introductions. The same goes for Willy – a description, no more. Willy, when he has got what he wants, proposes to fly straight back to England. Descriptions, gentlemen, however accurate, are a very long way from identifications, particularly from a frightened man. Of course we shall all wear gloves as a matter of course. I see no need for foolish disguises."

"I'm delighted to hear it," Charles Russell said.

"But you, sir, can be firmly *identified*. Van Loon knows you and he knows you're coming. I haven't presumed to make a plan for you." He sounded, for the first time worried, but the worry overlay respect. He might be the general giving his orders but Russell was the top class G One.

"I propose to stay here with Dame Molly Pegg."

"Did I hear that correctly?"

"Yes indeed."

The answer had surprised Dick Armitage; he thought it over quietly, then said:

"It would be impertinent to ask for an explanation."

"No, not at all – I'll explain myself gladly. As you say, Van Loon will certainly recognise me and he could give my name to the local police. But I feel confident he will not do so since I know too much to make that sensible. I've tried to put myself in his shoes, and as I see it what he'll fear above all things is being sent back to Holland to stand trial. Not for running away with the liquid assets – I doubt if they can touch him for that since under the very odd system he operated the money was probably legally his whomsoever it belonged to morally. If morally is an admissible word in what was clearly an amoral transaction. But he's in possession of a stolen painting and that Vermeer was not only stolen but looted. He knows I have somehow found that out and he thinks I am coming tonight to blackmail him. And so in a sense indeed I am. I don't want his money and I don't want his painting; I simply want a quiet holiday here, and I shall tell him that if he makes that difficult I can arrange for his extradition to Holland. The Dutch would like to forget the war but a looted Vermeer would be part of their heritage. They couldn't and wouldn't just turn a blind eye."

"Ingenious," Richard Armitage said. He walked to the window and looked out at the sea. It looked inviting in the morning sunlight but only a fool would risk a bathe. Pipes discharged into it every hundred yards. The travel brochures insisted noisily that all they carried was surface water but the locals raised a sceptical eyebrow. Besides, this was the open Atlantic and colder than the English Channel.

Dick Armitage returned to the table. "It's your risk," he said to Charles Russell, "not mine. Since the rest of us will all be away I haven't any ground to object to it. And in passing may I wish you good fortune." He tapped on the table. "I think that's all unless there are questions."

There were none and the four men rose together. Armitage said to Luiz Palmer:

"If you'd stay a moment, Luiz."

"Of course."

When Russell and Willy had shut the door Armitage said softly:

"Jan."

"You're worried about him?"

"Yes, a bit."

"I think I know what you mean. He's gone broody."

"It's a good enough word for a dangerous state. I'd have said he was rapt like a saint – ecstatic. You know the background of course?"

"I think I know most of it. Your maternal grandmother was worked to death but Jan's father died under interrogation. And I know what that means, I really do."

"So I've deliberately kept Jan outside. But there's one thing I should like you to do for me."

"Yes?"

"Make sure that he hasn't got a gun."

Charles Russell walked back to Dame Molly's villa where she gave him two gins and an excellent luncheon. He could see that she was seriously worried but he gave her high marks that she asked no questions. To Dame Molly all men were adult children. Unhappily one grew quite fond of them.

"What are you doing this afternoon?"

"After this marvellous lunch I shall sleep a bit."

"And after that?"

"I'm going out about six o'clock."

All Molly Pegg said was: "I'll see you off."

Charles Russell walked up the hill to the Villa Fleury. From time to time he looked at his watch. If he arrived too early he'd be conspicuous waiting and if he were late he could embarrass the others. The road was uphill but his stride still had spring in it. He was aware that he wasn't as young as he had been but he didn't entirely condemn himself that he still had a lively taste for adventure. The adrenalin in his system had risen.

He looked at his watch again: a hundred yards and one minute. Not bad. Behind him he could hear a vehicle. It passed him as he reached the gate, pulling up ten yards beyond it. Four men were in it but none of them looked at him.

Russell went to the gate and rang the bell. Nobody came out from the gatehouse but the speaker spluttered and then said clearly:

151

"Who's there, please?"

"Colonel Charles Russell. I have an appointment with Mijnheer Van Loon at half-past six."

"I have instructions to admit you. Wait."

First fence behind. Now the first piece of action.

There was a buzz from the electric lock and the speaker came to life again.

"Push the gate inwards."

Charles Russell pushed. Behind him he could hear the footfall of a man in rubber shoes running fast. As he went through he stumbled and fell, his body blocking the gate a yard open. There was a noisy oath from the porter's lodge and a man came out at a run.

Jan took him. Charles Russell saw an arm rise and fall, then the porter on his face on the ground. The other three men came through the gate. Armitage said respectfully: "Neat." Jan was dragging the gateman away and Willy blocking the gate with a stone. Charles Russell thought it all first-class drill. "Phase one," he said, "and it might have been worse." He was greatly addicted to understatement.

Armitage said: "Not to wait for Jan. He'll do what he has to and go back to the wagon. With your permission, sir, we will now try Phase two."

They went to the front door and Russell rang. Two short and two long, and for a long three seconds nothing happened. Then there was the same buzz in a lock but this time the door swung open on a spring. The four men went in in file, Luiz leading. They swung left into the study and stopped dead.

Karel van Loon hadn't risen to greet them. He was sitting in a chair without arms, cradling a World War Two machine pistol. The sling was over his shoulder correctly. "Colonel Russell I was expecting," he said, "and accordingly he will find a chair. You others, whoever you are, I was not. Accordingly you must need stay standing. I beg you not to move or try tricks."

Russell sat down in the single chair; he said conversationally: "I see you are armed. German-made spray gun."

"It was given me by my friends the Gestapo. They rightly

felt I needed it as protection against compatriots whose political views were not my own. I say rightly because I have used it twice. I would add that it's still in first-class condition."

"You're a pig," Luiz said, but the gun didn't move on him.

"And you, my friend are extremely naïve. As, in a different way, is the colonel, who has discovered that my Vermeer is genuine." It was hanging on the wall beside him but he didn't nod at it nor move his eyes. "So he comes here in an attempt at blackmail and since he's basically an orthodox man he's doing his thinking on orthodox lines. Which told him that in dealing with blackmailers a gun is an almost useless weapon. That line of thought is in this case wrong."

Charles Russell had been listening intently for their lives now depended on getting it right. You didn't change a man by giving him firearms but you could critically change his potential. Van Loon was in the driver's seat and his manner was increasingly confident. Russell had faced a gun before, held by men who had been even more arrogant. But this present bravado was super-ficial: beneath it lay an anxious amateur. A wrong move would draw a burst of fire but any distraction would break concentra-tion.

The trouble was he couldn't foresee one. Luiz Palmer had said he'd disarmed a man but not one with an automatic weapon. A single swinging burst would get them all.

Van Loon had begun to talk again; he was rubbing it in and greatly enjoying it.

"I had expected to kill a single man but three more will make little difference in principle. My relations with the police are excellent. I shall report an attempt at robbery with violence. Of course it may very well be said that in killing all four I over-reacted but in Portugal big money talks loudly. And since you are here as four, not one, I suspect you have also played into my hand. May I ask if you killed or disabled my gateman?"

Nobody answered: Van Loon sneered openly. "You see?" he said. "Real desperados. What else could I do but defend myself desperately?"

"You have it worked out," Charles Russell said coolly.

"If you concur in that let us end the talking." He started to move the pistol but too late. A man had come in at a crouching double. His hands were crooked like claws. He was screaming. He ran straight at Van Loon who said "Jan" unbelievingly. There was a burst of fire but an uncontrolled one. Plaster came down from a wall in a choking shower. Jan was trying to strangle Van Loon.

Luiz had sprung like a cat and as accurately. He was onto Van Loon in two lightning strides. The sling of the pistol had slipped from his shoulder and Luiz pulled it away from his lap. He looked at it for a moment and nodded, then he threw it into a corner in disgust. "Not a gentleman's weapon," he said contemptuously.

Jan was still strangling Karel van Loon and Luiz began to pull him away. He did it gently and with soothing words. "Later," he was saying. "Later." Finally he got them apart. Jan staggered and fell on the floor on his face. He was weeping and moaning and the fire had gone out of him.

Willy Smith found another chair for Armitage.

There was nearly a minute of total silence, broken only by the clamour from Jan. Russell ended it with a question to Armitage. "Was that planned too?"

"I confess it was not."

"Then the gods, whoever they be, have been kind."

"I suppose you could put it like that."

"I do."

Luiz was still standing by Karel van Loon. Van Loon had been slightly sick down his waistcoat. "Who are you?" he asked Armitage shakily.

"I'm the man who's been causing you trouble in Holland."

"God," Van Loon said. "Oh God. Oh God." Without a weapon he was back to impotence.

"And you're mistaken in thinking I'm here for blackmail. I'm here for every penny you have."

There was a last flare of forced and now febrile bravado. "That you may find it hard to reach."

"On the contrary you will open up for us. I don't think you

will stand much pain." He nodded towards Luiz. "Now. Gently at first. We're not his friends the Gestapo."

Luiz Palmer drew a peon's knife, looking at it reflectively, smiling. "The weapon of my race," he said. With a movement the eye could barely follow he cut Karel van Loon from eyebrow to chin. It wasn't deep, barely more than a nick, but Karel van Loon screamed in horror and outrage. He put up his hand and it came away red.

Dick Armitage went on talking collectedly. "That was only a threat or perhaps a promise. My friend can mark you for life and will. I gather you haven't much use for women but men will turn away as you pass them."

Van Loon said: "Animals. All of you animals."

"You may be right – that is not for me. But at least we don't sell men into slavery. We do not have them murdered by torture."

Karel van Loon stayed immobile, frozen. Armitage nodded at Luiz who raised the knife. Van Loon said: "No. No, no, no, no."

"Then open."

Fear chased greed across the bloodied face. Finally Van Loon said: "I cannot."

Luiz raised the knife again. A second's pause.

"The switches are behind the painting."

"My friend will walk behind you to the wall."

Van Loon got off his chair and almost fell. He recovered his balance and went to the picture. He took it off its hooks and lowered it. Behind was what looked like a miniature safe. Karel van Loon unlocked it with difficulty: his hands were trembling uncontrollably. Inside were three switches, all of them down. Van Loon threw all three up.

"There you are."

"Not quite. You are coming too. No nonsense." Armitage began to give his orders. "Van Loon goes first with our friend with the knife behind him. Be mindful that he can cut out your liver. I will go next and our other friend here brings up the rear. Colonel Russell, if he will be so good, will stay and keep an eye on Jan."

Who had risen and was propping a wall. The spasm had

passed, he looked utterly spent, but he had never taken his eyes from Van Loon.

The four men formed up in file and moved off and as the last of them went through the door Jan moved too. He went to the safe in the wall and looked in; to Russell he said in his terrible German: "They're marked but in English. I cannot read it. If there's justice in this world you must help me."

"Sometimes there's a sort of justice."

Russell had moved to the switches as he spoke. "They say *Strongroom* and *Safe* and the third *Protection*. All of them are now at OFF."

"Which of them is marked *Protection*?"

"The one on the left."

Jan promptly pulled it down to ON.

Russell was out of the room at once, running towards the sound of footsteps. From the head of the stairs which led down to the strongroom he could see that there were maybe twenty. The file of four men was halfway down. He called: "Stop!" and the last three men halted. All of them, though at different times, had heard a drill sergeant's voice and obeyed instinctively. But Van Loon looked over his shoulder, puzzled. This was some stupid English joke or maybe they were trying to mock him. He shrugged and went on, his hand on the banister.

There was a sudden hissing flash and he fell. For a moment his back had bent like a bow, then he rolled down the last of the stairs against the door.

Armitage turned and started to speak but for once Charles Russell cut him short. "I apologise for shouting rudely but there's been something a little unexpected. I'm going back to the study to put it right but until I give the all clear stand fast. On no account touch that banister. Wait."

He ran back to the study and threw the switch again, then went to the door and called out loudly. He thought it prudent not to leave Jan alone.

"Can you hear me from there?"

"Yes, quite clearly."

"It's safe to go on. I wish you luck."

He turned to Jan who was sitting quietly. On his face was a look of total peace. On the sideboard were a decanter and glasses and Russell poured a whisky thoughtfully. He said to Jan:

"Would you like a drink too?"

"No thank you. But a cigarette – "

"I'm sorry I don't have one. But a cigar?"

"If you'll be kind enough to cut and light it. I may look all right but I'm still pretty shaky."

Russell cut and lit a cigar meticulously, handing it to Jan in silence. Jan took three drags, inhaling deeply, then said to Russell:

"Could you have stopped me?"

"From changing that switch? I suppose I could. As you say yourself you were pretty shaky."

"But you didn't."

"Evidently."

"In that case I can only thank you."

Charles Russell drank his whisky slowly. The situation had its own fey humour. He had just allowed Jan to kill Karel van Loon and his conscience hadn't stirred as he'd done it. Well, moral judgments were never his forte and in any case Karel van Loon had been evil.

That thought, of course, was impermissible, logically a contradiction, but one could allow oneself the occasional luxury.

He sat down to await the return of the others.

The three men stepped over the body indifferently, still careful not to touch the banister. The door of the strongroom had opened already and they stood in a row in front of the safe. The same doubt was present in all three minds in spite of Charles Russell's call of all clear. Finally Armitage said:

"Let's toss. First man unpaired has to chance his arm."

They threw three coins and all came down tails. The next time Luiz and Willy were heads. Armitage picked up his Tails with a shrug. He walked to the safe and gripped the wheel. He spun it to the right. Nothing happened. He spun it to the left. The door opened.

Inside were four shelves, three packed with paper. On the fourth was a single leather-bound book.

Armitage put an arm inside, sweeping the lowest shelf's contents to the floor. It was a mixture of bearer bonds and currency. He picked up a bearer and nodded, satisfied. "High denomination Royal Dutch and the others will be the same sort of thing. But there's a lot more in cash than I thought he'd keep." He stirred it with a foot. "German and Swiss and even some English. No dollars, though – he knew his business. We're going to need at least two suitcases. Luiz, will you nip upstairs? If you can't find suitcases we'll have to use pillow slips."

Willy had been standing as still as a stone, his eyes on the single leather-bound book. Armitage asked him:

"Why don't you get it?"

"I thought I should let you go first."

"Very polite. And also cool."

"I feel anything but cool."

"Then get it."

Willy Smith took the book from the safe. It was heavy. He fluttered the pages and they fell open at L ... Mr and Mrs Alistair Leech. He had been holding his breath but now let it out softly. William Wilberforce Smith had his job back all right. He had it whenever he chose to demand it.

They packed Van Loon's loot and went back to the study. Russell and Jan were smoking in silence and Russell jerked his head at the suitcases. "Satisfactory?" he inquired.

"I think so. Of course we haven't had time to count but I'd be surprised if there was less than two million. And Willy has got what he wanted too."

He had been standing behind but now came forward. "It's dynamite, sir. Political dynamite."

"That's dangerous stuff. You must use it prudently."

"I'll do what I need to and nothing more." Willy looked at Dick Armitage, trying hard to be casual. "And now if you've no further use for me ..."

"None." Armitage and Willy Smith shook hands. "Be off with you and the best of luck."

Willy turned back to Russell. "Thank you, sir."

"For nothing. I like you."

Willy Smith went out with Luiz Palmer. Luiz was carrying the two big suitcases. Willy was almost running but not quite. He had to pick up his bag and call a taxi to the airport. Where he would buy the first free seat on offer.

Dick Armitage looked at Russell's drink. "I see you helped yourself."

"He owed it."

"I agree." Armitage poured one for himself and sat down. "What happened?" he asked.

Charles Russell told the story shortly.

"You thought fast."

"I had to."

Armitage took a pull at his drink. He was thinking that this was what Willy had told him. Charles Russell, in the pinches, would be more useful than a dozen strongarms. He looked over to Jan, still smoking silently. "Is he all right?"

"He's recovering from some sort of crisis. If I had to find a word for it I'd be inclined to 'exaltation'. But I wouldn't let him drive."

"Then *I* must. Jan drives as he plays polo – dangerously." Armitage took a second pull at his drink; he was visibly unwinding now. "Phase three," he said, "didn't go quite to plan and for your help in that I'm eternally grateful. But I see no reason to change phase four. The getaway can go as planned and you are now doubly safe with Dame Molly. Van Loon knew you all right but Van Loon is dead."

The Vermeer still stood on the ground against the wall. Dick Armitage rose and stood before it. Like Russell it made him feel physically sick . . . Betrayals. Sellings into slavery. Torture and death.

Russell asked softly: "You're taking that too?"

"I am. But I wouldn't give it space in my house for any sum

you may care to mention. I'm going to give it back where it belongs."

"And where is that?"

"In the Rijksmuseum. It was looted from an elderly Jewish widow. She was childless and had bequeathed it there."

"An act of very delicate conscience."

"Only partly that. It is also insurance. It's conceivable the Dutch could make trouble for me – after all Van Loon was still one of their nationals. I don't see exactly what they could do but if a famous painting comes back to Holland my bet is that they won't do a thing. I'm half Dutch myself and I know how they think."

"You'd have done well on the General Staff," Russell said.

Dick Armitage picked the painting up and Russell gave an arm to Jan. The station wagon was already loaded, Luiz standing beside it, waiting for orders. Dick Armitage added the picture and shut the back doors.

"You said I would make a good staff officer and I'm going to presume on that commendation."

"Presume away."

"You are still wearing gloves."

"Why so I am." Charles Russell took them off and they all shook hands.

"It's been a pleasure to meet you, sir."

"I feel the same."

Russell watched them drive away but not for long.

At dinner Dame Molly was decidedly jumpy. She wasn't a woman who pestered with questions so she put it as a simple statement.

"You might have asked me before you took my gloves."

"You noticed?"

"Of course. I needed them to cook this dinner which I hope you'll agree is better than average. When I needed them they weren't there. Now they are."

"I apologise," Charles Russell said.

His matter-of-factness stung her Scots temper. "You've been out on a job," she snapped.

"You could call it that."

"What in God's name made you do it at your age?"

He thought for some time before he answered. "Perhaps a sense of natural justice."

"I didn't think you had such a thing."

"Nor did I."

15

Charles Russell wasn't the only man who occasionally indulged in a luxury but in Willy's case the rare self-clemency had not been an illogical thought; it had been the material fact of first-class travel by air. The meal had been slightly over-presented and the steward uncomfortably close to fussy but Willy had dozed without disturbance. The ledger was in a briefcase on his lap.

At Heathrow he went through Customs unchallenged and was waiting for a taxi when a policeman walked up and touched his arm. "Mr William Wilberforce Smith?"

"I am." Willy's heart had turned over twice but now settled. The policeman had saluted politely, a courtesy very seldom offered if there were anything even mildly wrong.

"Mr Pallant would like a word with you, sir."

The 'sir' clinched it and Willy relaxed some more. "I don't think I know Mr Pallant except by name."

"I was to tell you he's still Colonel Russell's friend. Also that he has sent a car for you."

The policeman was a cricket fan and they chatted throughout the drive to London. At the ugly headquarters another policeman took over, ushering Willy to Pallant's room.

"Kind of you to come," he said. He waved at a chair and they both sat down. Jack Pallant was in plain clothes and he wore them well. He had a smile which split his face like a melon and large and slightly prominent teeth. He looked like a vaguely amiable crocodile awaiting some especial titbit, but the amiability hid a formidable shrewdness. Willy had often heard Russell speak of him and he knew that he wasn't a man to try to fool. On the other hand he played his cards fairly. The question was what cards they were. Why had he sent for Willy at all? He decided he would take the initiative.

"How did you know I was on that flight?"

"Because I had you tailed to Portugal." Pallant held up a hand. "There's no cause for alarm. To be accurate I had Armitage tailed and you, Willy Smith, accompanied Armitage."

"I see."

"No you don't – you don't see at all. Permit me to make my position clear. I like to know where Armitage *is* – he is that sort of man as I'm sure you'll agree – but his operations abroad are not my business." Pallant produced his saurian smile. "I'll be frank and put it rather more forcibly. The less I know of his doings abroad the happier a British policeman I am. So I had him shadowed to Estoril but I gave no instructions to report on his actions. I know he has left his hotel and that is all. Putting it coarsely that keeps my nose clean. But you, Willy Smith, went with Armitage. Why? I should add I have heard that you've lost your job."

"You hear things," Willy said.

"When I want to."

Willy, too, could think fast and did so. "So you wondered if I'd gone in with Armitage?"

Again the saurian smile. "The thought had occurred."

"I haven't joined his gang and don't mean to."

"I'm glad of that. Then why go with him?"

"Perhaps for a holiday."

"Boy, come off it."

Willy couldn't help smiling: this man was good. He was tough but had a reputation for fairness. "May I have a cup of tea?"

"By all means. And time to think. That's perfectly in order. I'll join you."

They drank their tea and Pallant smoked. Willy put the empty cup down.

"I'll put it this way since you oblige me to do so. I haven't gone in with Armitage permanently but I mean to get my own job back again. So there was a mutual but quite temporary interest. Armitage did his business in Portugal and I was careful to mind my own."

"Which was connected with getting your job back?"

"Yes."

Jack Pallant said: "You were wasting your time. You can start again on Monday."

"What?"

"I said you could start on Monday and so you can."

"Somebody has fixed it with Laver?"

"Laver isn't there to be fixed. Did you see the English papers on this holiday in Estoril?" Willy shook his head and Pallant went on. "There's been a bit of a shuffle in Number Ten. The Prime Minister has been rocky for months – the Lefties are after his blood in full cry. So he's bought himself a bit of time – changes in the Cabinet and so on. One of the so ons was Richard Laver. He wasn't a strong man but he was conscientious. The Left wanted something much more pliable. So out he has gone."

"He was sacked?"

"Not quite. I'd prefer to say he's been kicked upstairs. *Stellenbosched* my grandfather called it. They've given him something in race relations and to be fair to him he'll do it admirably."

"And the new man will take me back?"

"He will."

"You're perfectly sure?"

"I'm the new man."

It was less than polite to have shown astonishment but Pallant merely showed his teeth again. "I know what you're thinking perfectly. Perfectly. A policeman in the Executive? Nonsense. But if you stop to think it isn't quite nonsense, or not in the present political climate. Détente and all that spurious rubbish. The CIA much diminished, pinkos everywhere. Policemen are traditionally neutral, they're paid to uphold the law and respect it. Which will suit the Left very well indeed." An eyelid dropped for a moment sardonically. "So I'm just what the doctor ordered temporarily. And personally it suits me well. There's another job I'd like much better but my boss isn't that much older than I am and humanly speaking I'll never get it. So I'm accepting the Executive happily.

I dare say I won't last very long for what they want is a stooge and I'm not cut out for one. There may be some rather rough riding from time to time." The manner changed suddenly: he was giving an order. "And now that you're working for me I can ask it. What have you got in that damned great briefcase?"

"May I have another tea?"

"You may not. Tea rots the guts – just look at Indians. But take all the time you want to think. I gather you don't drink. I do." He poured a gin and tonic and waited.

It didn't take Willy Smith very long. He'd been taught to eschew what wasn't relevant and the basic facts were stark and simple. Willy was carrying political dynamite but he had never intended to use it politically; he had intended to use it to get his job back. Which Jack Pallant had just given him freely; he had made no terms, he'd been friendly and generous. And Jack Pallant had said that he wasn't a stooge, something which Willy knew already; he had spoken of occasional rough riding. What Willy was carrying was now useless to Willy but it might well be very useful to Pallant. He said at length:

"Have you heard of Van Loons?"

"I know what they do."

"This briefcase contains their private ledger. The names on it are extremely interesting. Amongst them a Mr Alistair Leech in the sum of eight hundred thousand pounds."

It was Pallant's turn to take time to think. Finally he said: "That's a blockbuster. What are you going to do with it?"

"What *was* I going to do with it?"

"That I can guess. What *are* you going to do with it?"

"Give it to you."

"On what terms?"

"No terms. You could call it an act of appreciation."

He held out the briefcase to Pallant who took it, locking it in a safe with some care. Pallant returned to Willy Smith. "It's a pity you don't drink," he said.

"I have something better to do."

"Go and do it. But don't be late on Monday morning."

He sat down with his crocodile grin and another gin . . . A good boy, that, a potential highflyer. Charles Russell had thought well of him and that had been enough for Pallant. And Charles Russell's opinion had just been confirmed. Willy might well have committed some crime but in the Executive resource rated higher; he'd thought fast and he'd been gracefully generous. It wasn't quite impossible that one day he would sit in Russell's chair. How old was he? Say the early thirties. Give Pallant four years and he might still be too young, but some day, one day . . . His colour wouldn't go against him: there would be people who would mistakenly cheer. Mistakenly because if Willy made it he would do so on his merit not his skin.

Besides Karel van Loon and Leech himself only two other people had known his arrangements. One had been Phyllis, the other his broker, and it was his stockbroker who now brought the news to him. He did it on the telephone, more than a little put out and excited. He'd been telephoning Amsterdam all the morning for the banking world was boiling over. Rumours were flying as thick as dust and many were no doubt discountable but there were one or two facts and they didn't look pretty. Karel van Loon had disappeared and no payment of income had been made for some days. It was rumoured that he had gone to Spain, to Argentina, even to Iceland. His bank was still open for routine business but that had never been large and was mostly a front. But he himself had unquestionably gone and it was known he'd been selling gold in the market. The stockbroker passed this news with an acid relish. He took the *Telegraph* and the *Financial Times* and had never much cared for Mr Alistair Leech. He ended with a cautious disclaimer. Nothing was certain but it didn't look good.

Leech agreed quietly that it didn't look good.

Surprisingly quietly he thought, as he put down the telephone. It had been true the idea had come from Phyllis, and though he wasn't a man of conscience he had known an enormous risk when it stared at him. The loss of that money would tear her to pieces but it wouldn't quite do that to himself. She had called his pension piddle; it was not. It provided a modest sufficiency, and on top of that he had for once been fortunate. He had been offered what was called the presidency of one of the minor Cambridge colleges. It had a tradition of progressive thinking or it wouldn't have offered the post to Leech. Poor old Puttock had once been an undergraduate. The salary was less than princely but a house went with it and well-trained servants. It was a dignified retreat from reality and had another and substantial advantage. Phyllis would loathe the idea of Cambridge. If his luck held she might even refuse to come.

He left a note for her that they'd lost their capital, then took a taxi to his titled doctor.

But it wasn't the sort of consultation which Phyllis Leech had once thought probable, not a step in a carefully planned campaign which would end in a discreet announcement that the Prime Minister's health had broken down and accordingly he must retire from politics. For he wasn't going to retire – not yet. He had bought himself another year by the expedient of almost total surrender. Peters had been moved from the Home Office and Puttock retired to a misty oblivion. Neither move had caused any stir but the fact that the Ginger Job was now in the Cabinet had not been missed by political journalists. Comment had been pithy and varied. A few had applauded – 'broadening the democratic base' – and rather more had deplored it openly. Nearly all had seen the humiliation, for the Ginger Job's terms had been more than a place. He had always mistrusted Richard Laver, less for what he had done, perhaps, than for the fact that he wasn't an open ally, and he had demanded that he be publicly sacked. Alistair Leech had for once stood firm. He wouldn't sack Laver but he would kick him upstairs. And Phyllis Leech had this time been right. There'd been a job in the race relations racket and Laver was going to start there on Monday.

So Leech drove to his doctor in very fair heart. Normally these annual check-ups were matters of half an hour at most – heart, lungs and blood pressure. Urine. Out. This had been done a week ago but this time there had been X-rays and blood tests. These had in no way frightened Leech, since like Russell he thought little of doctors. They had a superlative system of cover-up and, especially when in fashionable practice, they liked to share the trough with their brethren. So there'd been X-rays and blood tests and other mysteries and they'd told him to come back in a week.

Today there had been a second man present, a stout little dumpling in horn-rimmed glasses. Alistair Leech didn't catch his name. His own doctor had a pompous manner and now he said at the top of his form:

"My colleague and I are entirely agreed. We think you should take much more care of your health. There are signs you've been overdoing things lately."

"You're telling me I'm not as young as I used to be?"

"Yes," the dumpling said. "More or less."

Alistair Leech was suddenly angry. He was tolerant of restrictive practices but this was going too far. They had taken him.

"I could have told you that myself at less cost."

He told the official car to follow him, walking in the sun towards Oxford Street. It began to thaw his chagrin slowly. He had almost certainly lost a fortune but the income had mostly been spent by Phyllis. She had threatened to leave him and now she would. She might conceivably have flounced out already and that would really make his day. Meanwhile he had bought a year more of office, and after that the delights of Cambridge.

But Phyllis hadn't flounced out; she hadn't dared. She had been doing her sums and they hadn't come out right. She had a little money still invested in England but a good deal of expensive jewellery; and she hadn't been naïve enough to suppose that when it came to selling jewellery you got anything like the price some man had paid. But the difference, allowing for increased values, had come as a disagreeable surprise. She had totted up her assets and had frowned. Translated into terms of living they represented a small flat in an unfashionable quarter, a Mini and of course no maid, and to Phyllis Leech this was middle-class poverty.

She rang up John's office and waited confidently. He had always put business aside to talk to her. "I'd like to speak to Mr John Delaney."

A woman's voice said: "I'm afraid he's away."

"Can you say for how long?"

"I'm afraid I can't."

"I'm Mrs Alistair Leech."

A silence, then simply: "Oh." Phyllis froze. There had been something about the exclamation which had told her more than a dozen sentences. This secretary had been briefed to deal with her.

"Can you say where he has gone?"

"To Florida."

"Did he leave an address?"

"Not for general use, madam."

Phyllis put down the phone in a fury. She poured a stiff drink and fought for control. When she had it she went to her bedroom and stripped, standing before the bevelled mirror. For her age she still had a marvellous figure but there were portents about her eyes and neck. Her masseuse had begun making minatory noises.

She wondered who John's new woman was, probably that highbrow actress whom once he'd been foolish enough to mention. She worked in one of those way-out reps which specialised in sociological bowelbinders.

She looked at her body again. Men were stupid.

But she was a realist and could face reality. I'm old man's meat, she thought, or very young. A young man might take her and be flattered to do so, but young men very seldom had money, and old men could be distinctly tricky. They had sons and sometimes even grandsons; they were difficult to part from their assets.

She dressed and went back to her desk to think. She had read her husband's note with blank horror and had been relishing tearing the fool to pieces. But she realised that might now be risky: their positions had been subtly reversed. By becoming what she thought of as poor he had become, in a very real sense, her master. She knew that he'd bought a year of office at the price of a public humiliation and she knew about the offer from Cambridge. So she'd have to stick with Alistair after all.

Cambridge, she thought – it sounded terrible. But it would also have one grim advantage. So she wouldn't tongue-lash her husband, she'd be forgiving and gentle. But she would go with him to that Cambridge college and there she would make his life intolerable.

She never did so – the great fixer slipped her. Behind Leech's back the two doctors shrugged. "I'm glad he cut us short as he did. I detest the usual spiel, don't you?"

"He was certainly pretty brusque."

"He was rude."

"He's not a nice man."

"What politico is?"

The stout one flicked through a pile of X-rays. "You agree that it's quite inoperable?"

"Totally."

"How long would you give him?"

"Perhaps six months."

"I'd put it nearer three myself."

Sir Richard Laver was quietly contented for he was back at work he understood. He had lost a quite substantial allowance and the change had been made with brutal abruptness but it was possible to persuade oneself that the compensations outweighed the losses.

The file now on his desk, for instance. It was entitled *Mrs Mary Small (Writing as Marganita Loveday)* and it appeared that she wrote with great success. She wasn't one of the significant sisters but wrote stories about doctors and nurses or secretaries who married their bosses, and she had never been seriously reviewed in her life. This didn't annoy her since she was a sensible woman, and in any case she was quietly aware that she made vastly more money than the so-sensitives added together and doubled. They looked down on her from their bleak frugality while she did four or five books a year and flourished.

And this admirable woman had advertised for a secretary. She had detailed her requirements meticulously, adding at the end 'must be white', and an ad-editor with a morning hangover had somehow let it go past him into print.

Immediately the balloon rose vertically. The tender consciences and the human righters were instantly after the lady's blood, and the file was now three inches thick. Any ordinary man would have sent for the shredder, but Laver wasn't an ordinary man, he was a conscientious civil servant. He had read the monstrous thing through with care – the correspondence, the minuting, the whole soggy pudding. Now it was on his desk for decision.

Difficult, he thought – very tricky. It was certain there'd been a breach of the law but it was doubtful if it had been deliberate and there wasn't any suggestion of malice. Would not a stiff letter of solemn reproof serve better than the law's dimmed majesty? The Department's lawyer had of course been consulted but he had confined himself to his proper field, which had been to advise that the law had been broken and that a conviction was as near to certainty as the whims of ageing judges allowed. But whether or not to prosecute was a matter for the Administrative mandarins.

Whom he privately thought a race of madmen.

Sir Richard Laver wasn't mad and he had heard of taking sledgehammers to nuts. But unhappily one of the Sunday heavies had taken up the case and run it. There had been a thunderous leader which had used the word 'outrage', and on another page and a different Sunday a barely non-libellous pint of acid on the opus of Marganita Loveday. On top of that there'd been a question in Parliament.

Sir Richard Laver made his mind up. He didn't dare not to act so he did. He wrote 'Prosecute' on the file and went to lunch. He went to his slightly grubby club where he allowed himself a half-carafe of table wine. He didn't often drink at luncheon but he thought he had earned it by doing his duty.

Above him a recording angel made an entry in a long, long column. The column was headed simply *Self Interest*.

If Laver had been quietly contented Jane Lightwater was actively happy. The *hetairai*, she knew, often married well, and she was in the classic tradition. It was an overworked word but for once used correctly. She had slipped into county life like a second skin. Not a soul had known her in darkest Northamptonshire but her manner had made her at once acceptable. Already they'd dined with the local bigwigs.

Piet had slotted in beautifully too. A Dutchman crazy on hunting the fox had been a welcome new topic at boring parties, and Piet had been in England long enough to know the main trap which the Dutch put their feet in. A clanger was a clanger and the English would look the other way; you could be as blunt as you pleased and mostly survive it but you mustn't pretend that what they thought was a defect was in fact an especial virtue of your own. You mustn't think of them as devious, or if that were impossible, never show it.

So Jane Lightwater sang as she cooked his lunch. *Oh, what a beautiful morning.*

It was.

He came in presently dressed up for riding. It wasn't hunting time yet, not even cubbing, but he had come for a weekend's hacking and pleasure. He was a man who liked to do things correctly and he was wearing a fine broadcloth jacket, a stock and a reinforced bowler hat. The hat was in his hand. He had broken it.

"I tried a fence," he said. "I fell down."

She kissed him and took away the hat. "Smashing morning?" she asked.

He was puzzled at first but got it quickly. "Ha!" he said; he slapped his thigh. "English joke. I'm getting good at them."

"You're good at other things too."

"You please me."

Charles Russell and Molly Pegg were at dinner. He could see that she was tensed up again but he knew she would tell him the reason in time. She did so over coffee outside.

"Have you seen the local English paper?"

"I didn't know there was one."

"It has a story about a big robbery here, a grand villa up on the hill, a Dutchman. Apparently he was a bit of a recluse and when the maid arrived in the morning she couldn't get in. She called the police who broke in somehow, and there was the gateman tied up like a parcel. Inside in the study there was a weapon and bullet marks but there wasn't any sign of blood. But downstairs the Dutchman was dead, electrocuted. His strongroom was open and so was his safe. Everything had been taken. Everything."

"A professional job," Charles Russell said.

"The Dutchman's name was Karel van Loon."

"I've met him. He's the son of the man we saw in Amsterdam."

She hesitated before speaking again. She didn't expect the whole story nor want it but there was one thing she must know.

"Did you kill him?"

He said with truth but less than candour: "I didn't touch him the whole of that evening. Nor did I plan to have him killed."

"Is that the truth?"

"I'm a lousy liar."

"Yes," she said, satisfied. "Yes, you are." Since he was answering she risked her next question. "But surely he must have recognised you?"

"He did. Equally surely the man is dead."

"So you're not at any risk staying on here?"

"If I were I wouldn't be risking you too."

She said with a hint of irritation: "If it was money you had only to ask me."

"You're a very nice woman."

"I am to my friends."

"In any case it wasn't money."

"What was it, then?"

"I told you once."

"Some nonsense about a sense of justice?"

"I dislike repetition. Let's go to bed."

Dame Molly undressed with deliberation. She was thinking again that all men were children but that life could be very dull without one.

Charles Russell took a reflective bath and halfway through it he laughed aloud. He had remembered that he'd been thanked three times. The first had been for his valued help in entering with intent to steal; the second had been for his valued help in arming William Wilberforce Smith with the means to blackmail

Sir Richard Laver; and the third had been for the negative act of allowing a switch to be thrown back to ON. All these were in fact quite serious crimes but he was going to sleep eight hours without stirring.

Willy had taken Amanda dancing again. It had been a gala night with a visiting band, and the noise had been more than usually deafening. Willy had brought his own car and drove her home. On the steps she said:

"Father and mother are back."

"I know." It was disappointing but it couldn't be helped.

"Mama has ideas for a rather grand wedding. That's going to mean delay."

"I know."

She looked deliberately at the ring on her finger. It had once belonged to Phyllis Leech and at the fashionable jeweller it had come from that morning it had cost Willy Smith about three times more than Phyllis had received for its sale. He saw Amanda's glance and raised his eyebrows.

"One ring's as good as another," she told him.

"Not at two in the morning it isn't."

"Why not?"

"Because if we went to my flat we might be seen and because no hotel would take us in."

"They would in Brighton."

"Brighton?" Willy Smith was astonished. It wasn't, to his mind, where you took a princess. "It's full of shonks," he said at length.

"Which means there are hotels with night clerks."

"Would they take us in?"

"You must be joking."

"What's your father going to say?"

"What can he? You've got your job back. I'm twenty-two. Are you afraid of him?"

"Yes, a bit. And I'm not carrying a lot of money."

"I am," she said. She waved her handbag.

He laughed but he was also impressed. She was going to make a marvellous wife. "So you had it all worked out," he said.

"Sometimes you're a bit of a dumbo."

They went back to the car and drove to Brighton.